"So," Clint said, "will they be waiting outside for me?"

"Juanito will want to," Rodrigo said. "He will want to face you alone, and know that he killed the Gunsmith."

"Why don't you do me a favor and go take a look?" Clint said.

"*Sí, señor.*" Rodrigo headed for the door.

"No," Clint said, "don't go to the door. Look out a window."

"Oh, *sí, señor.*"

Rodrigo changed directions and headed for a window. He peered out, taking care not to be seen from outside.

"They are not there, *señor.*"

"What do you think that means?"

Rodrigo turned from the window to look at him.

"Señor Montoya probably would not allow Juanito to wait for you."

"He's a smart man," Clint said. "What would he do?"

"He would probably wait until he had more men before he came after you."

"And why would he come after me?" Clint asked. "We never met until today."

"Well . . . you are the Gunsmith, *señor,*" Rodrigo said. "Is that not enough reason for most men?"

Clint sighed.

"Unfortunately, it is—most of the time."

DON'T MISS THESE
ALL-ACTION WESTERN SERIES
FROM THE BERKLEY PUBLISHING GROUP

THE GUNSMITH by J. R. Roberts

Clint Adams was a legend among lawmen, outlaws, and ladies. They called him . . . the Gunsmith.

LONGARM by Tabor Evans

The popular long-running series about Deputy U.S. Marshal Custis Long—his life, his loves, his fight for justice.

SLOCUM by Jake Logan

Today's longest-running action Western. John Slocum rides a deadly trail of hot blood and cold steel.

BUSHWHACKERS by B. J. Lanagan

An action-packed series by the creators of Longarm! The rousing adventures of the most brutal gang of cutthroats ever assembled—Quantrill's Raiders.

DIAMONDBACK by Guy Brewer

Dex Yancey is Diamondback, a Southern gentleman turned con man when his brother cheats him out of the family fortune. Ladies love him. Gamblers hate him. But nobody pulls one over on Dex . . .

WILDGUN by Jack Hanson

The blazing adventures of mountain man Will Barlow—from the creators of Longarm!

TEXAS TRACKER by Tom Calhoun

J.T. Law: the most relentless—and dangerous—manhunter in all Texas. Where sheriffs and posses fail, he's the best man to bring in the most vicious outlaws—for a price.

THE GUNSMITH

395

THE THREE MERCENARIES

J. R. ROBERTS

JOVE BOOKS, NEW YORK

THE BERKLEY PUBLISHING GROUP
Published by the Penguin Group
Penguin Group (USA) LLC
375 Hudson Street, New York, New York 10014

USA • Canada • UK • Ireland • Australia • New Zealand • India • South Africa • China

penguin.com

A Penguin Random House Company

THE THREE MERCENARIES

A Jove Book / published by arrangement with the author

For information, address: The Berkley Publishing Group,
a division of Penguin Group (USA) LLC,
375 Hudson Street, New York, New York 10014.

ISBN: 978-0-515-15498-6

PUBLISHING HISTORY
Jove mass-market edition / November 2014

PRINTED IN THE UNITED STATES OF AMERICA

10 9 8 7 6 5 4 3 2 1

Cover illustration by Sergio Giovine.

ONE

The dead cowboy was carried into the saloon and set down on the bar.

"Where's the judge?" one of the men asked.

"He's comin'," the bartender said. "Just leave 'im."

The three men who carried the body into the saloon looked at the bartender.

"Any chance we can get a drink?" one of them asked.

"Yeah, sure," the bartender said. "One shot for each of you."

He poured three shots of red-eye, and the three men tossed them down.

"Okay," the bartender said, "now get out before the judge comes out."

"Ain't he gonna want the body moved when he's done?" another man asked.

"Yeah, but we'll get somebody else to do it." He knew the three men were angling for another free drink. They slunk out of the saloon.

The bartender studied the dead cowboy. He looked like he was in his thirties, had apparently been shot through the chest. His gun was still in his holster. He was about to go through the dead man's pockets when the judge appeared.

The judge was a tall man in his sixties, with white hair. He was wearing a soiled white shirt and a pair of suspenders. He had his gavel in his hand.

"Judge," the bartender said.

The judge nodded at him. When the saloon became his courtroom, the bartender became his bailiff.

"Go through his pockets yet?" the judge asked.

"I was about to do that."

"Then do it."

As the bartender went through the pockets, the judge took out a pair of wire-framed glasses and perched them on the end of his nose. He watched as the man went into all the pockets, turned them inside out, and came out with . . .

"Forty dollars," the bartender/bailiff said. "Guess he wasn't robbed."

The judge came closer, leaned over, and studied the wound in the man's chest.

"Somebody didn't like him."

"I guess."

The judge looked at the forty dollars in the bartender's hand, then examined the body again.

The bartender jumped in surprise as the judge slammed his gavel down on the bar.

"Forty dollars for carrying a concealed weapon."

"Him?" the bartender asked. "Concealed?"

"Forty dollars."

The bartender/bailiff looked down at the money in his hands. "He just happens to have that much on him," he said, handing the money over.

"Sell his gun," the judge said, "and have the body taken to the undertaker."

"Yes, sir."

The judge counted the money in his hands just to be sure, then slammed his gavel down again and said, "Court's adjourned!"

"Drink?" the bartender asked, now relieved of his job as bailiff.

"I said court's adjourned, didn't I?" the judge asked peevishly. "Do I have to repeat myself?" He raised his gavel.

"No sir!"

The judge turned and walked away.

The judge entered his office and sat in front of his ancient roll-top desk. He took the money out of his pocket, opened the top drawer, and deposited it. The town of Langtry, Texas, did not yet have a bank. He sat back in his chair, lit a cigar, and sipped his drink.

Judge Roy Bean much preferred his Jersey Lily as a saloon than a courtroom.

TWO

Clint Adams left San Antonio, Texas, ahead of trouble. It had become obvious to him that there were several men there who were working up the nerve to try him. Eventually, they might even have decided to join forces against him. His best bet was to leave town, since he was pretty much finished with San Antonio anyway.

Normally he wouldn't leave town ahead of trouble. He wouldn't want it to get around that Clint Adams ran away from trouble, but he didn't consider this running. This was avoidance. But if they followed him, he'd have no choice but to deal with them.

It took Clint three days to reach Acuña, Mexico. His plan was to spend a few days there—just over the border—and then ride north. Eventually, he'd reach Labyrinth, his home away from . . . well, the only place he could call home. And yet the thing he liked about it was that while it remained the same in his absence, there were always slight changes upon his return.

As he rode into Acuña, he found it a small, sleepy town— a village actually. He'd been checking his back trail religiously, and hadn't seen any sign that he was being followed.

So he felt fairly certain he'd be able to spend an easy day or two there.

He took Eclipse to the livery, got his room in the small hotel. It was simple, a small bed, an old dresser, and a wooden chair. But it was remarkably clean, which was unusual for a small, dusty town like Acuña.

But what he was looking forward to was some good Mexican food. He went down to the small space that could hardly be called a hotel lobby, and approached the front desk.

The clerk was a Mexican in his forties, with slicked-down hair and a well-cared-for mustache.

"Can I help you, *señor?*"

"Who makes the best food in town?"

"Ah, *señor*," the clerk said, "you want to go across the street to Carmelita's Cantina."

"I'm looking for good enchiladas and tacos," Clint said.

"Whatever she makes is the best in town, *señor*," the clerk assured him. "You tell her Paco sent you over."

"I'll tell her," Clint said. "*Gracias, señor.*"

"*Por nada, señor!*"

Clint left the hotel and walked across the street to Carmelita's Cantina.

As he entered, he saw that the place had a small bar and four tables, and that was it. None of the tables were being used, which was not necessarily a good indication of a place's food, but it was a small town and it was not supper time. And the smells in the air were fabulous.

A small man wearing an apron came out of the kitchen and smiled broadly. Because he was so small—perhaps five feet tall—it was hard to gauge his age. He could have been thirty or fifty.

"*Señor*, welcome to Carmelita's." He smiled broadly, showing a couple of gold teeth.

"I heard you have the best food in town."

"*Sí, señor*," the man said. "We have that honor. Would you like a table?"

"If you can fit me in."

The man laughed and said, "Ah, the *señor* is funny." He waved magnanimously. "You may choose any table you like."

"I'll take that one," Clint said, pointing to the one that was farthest from the door.

"Excellent choice!"

The small man led Clint to the table, then asked, "Would the *señor* like something to drink?"

"*Cerveza*," Clint said.

"*Sí, señor*," the man said, "I will bring the beer right away. And to eat?"

"Burritos, enchiladas, tacos, and rice," Clint said. "And anything else you can think of."

"Ah, the *señor* has a large appetite," the man said happily. "I will tell Carmelita and she will begin the cooking."

"You mean there really is a Carmelita?"

"Oh, *sí, señor*," the man said with a broad smile. "She is the cook, and she is *mi esposa*."

"Well, congratulations."

"Oh, *señor*, we have been married a very long time," the man said, "but *gracias*."

The man hurried away and quickly returned with a mug of beer. After that he kept coming back with platters of enchiladas, burritos, tacos, and lots of Spanish rice and refried beans. The last trip back and forth from the kitchen brought Clint a large pile of tortillas. He piled the food into tortillas, rolled them up, and ate happily. He didn't know if the food was the best in town, but he couldn't imagine there was better.

"What's your name?" he asked the waiter when he brought him another mug of beer.

"Rodrigo."

"Rodrigo, tell your wife this food is delicious," he told the man.

"I will tell her, *señor*. She will be very, very pleased," the man said. "*Muchas gracias*."

Clint nodded and waved, his mouth full, and the man ran happily back to the kitchen.   •

While he was eating, three men entered the cantina and went to the bar. They were all Mexican and looked over at Clint with interest, then had a conversation at the bar with Rodrigo. It was in Spanish, but Clint could tell he was the subject. If they were looking for trouble, he hoped they would wait until after he had eaten.

Alas, they did not.

THREE

The three men turned to look at Clint, with beer mugs in their hands. Clint was eating his last taco, and wanted to enjoy it just as much as the first.

"Hey, *gringo!*" one of the men yelled.

Clint closed his eyes. It apparently was not going to happen.

"Are you talking to me?" he asked.

"Am I talkin' to you?" the man asked. He spoke very thickly accented English, which sounded like "Am I talkin' to joo?" He laughed, exchanged glances with his two compadres, and then said, "I don' see anybody else in here, do joo?"

"No," Clint said, "I just couldn't believe you were talking to me, since we don't know each other."

"Oh, I see," the man said. "Well, we can fix dat, eh? My name is Juanito. What is jours?"

Now Clint knew one of two things could happen if he gave the man his real name. He could dissuade them and send them packing, or it could encourage them to try him. They all had bandoliers across their chests, pistols in holsters, and rifles that were currently leaning against the bar.

"My name is Clint."

"Cleent?" the man said. "What kind of name is Cleent?"

"I don't know," Clint said. "What kind of name is Juanito? Isn't that a girl's name?"

The smile disappeared from the man's face.

"What? You are calling Juanito a woman?"

"Just commenting on your name," Clint said. "Isn't that what you were doing?"

"Juanito," Rodrigo said from behind the bar, "the *señor* meant no disrespect. Please, no trouble, eh?"

One of the other men put his hand on Juanito's arm, raised his other hand to Rodrigo, and said, "No, no, Rodrigo, fear not. There will be no trouble." He was older than the other two, and for the first time Clint thought he might be looking at a father or an uncle, with two younger sons or nephews.

"Please, *señor*," the man said to Clint, "you must forgive my son. He has a poor way of showing his curiosity."

"No problem," Clint said. "I'll just finish my meal."

"Rodrigo," the older man said, "please take the *señor* another *cerveza*, from me."

"*Sí*, Señor Montoya," Rodrigo said.

"Please," Montoya said, "finish your meal in peace."

"*Gracias*," Clint said, "and thank you for the beer."

"*Por nada*," the older man said. He and his two younger comrades turned back to the bar, but Juanito was not happy.

Rodrigo brought the second beer over to Clint, who popped the last of the taco into his mouth.

"Rodrigo," he said, "please give Carmelita my compliments."

"Would you like to tell her yourself?" Rodrigo asked. "That would please her very much."

"I would be happy to."

"Good, good," Rodrigo said, "thank you. I will get her."

Montoya and one of his comrades kept their backs to Clint while they drank their own beer, but Juanito kept peering over his shoulder. Clint figured he wasn't out of the woods yet as far as trouble in Acuña went. Maybe he should just move on now that he'd eaten.

Rodrigo reappeared with a large, heavy woman in tow. She was easily twice his size, towering over him, but had the same wide smile on her face. They seemed to be a very happy couple.

"*Señor*, this is my Carmelita," Rodrigo said.

"*Señor*," she said. "I am happy to meet you."

"The pleasure is mine, *señora*," Clint said. "Your food has brought joy to my heart—and to my stomach."

The couple laughed and she thanked him profusely. Carmelita's skin was like smooth, light chocolate, and despite her size, she was pleasant looking, almost pretty—especially when she smiled.

"I should get going—" he started, but Rodrigo took hold of his right wrist.

"No," he said, "stay for *café*. You will like Carmelita's coffee." He leaned closer and said, "Do not leave until they do."

"All right," Clint said. "I'll have some coffee."

"Excellent."

"I will get it!" Carmelita said, and hurried back to the kitchen as quickly as her bulk would allow her.

FOUR

Carmelita brought the coffee out and sat with Clint while he drank it. It was excellent. Rodrigo went to the bar to see if the three men wanted another beer, but they didn't. They paid for what they'd drunk, and left. Juanito threw one last hard look Clint's way.

Rodrigo came back to the table and sat down. He said something to Carmelita, and she rose and went back to the kitchen.

"So?" Clint asked.

"That was Señor Montoya and his two sons, Juanito and Pablo," Rodrigo said.

"And?"

"They are bad men."

"Señor Montoya seemed to be very . . . sensible."

"That is because he knew who you were."

"Did you tell him?"

"Me?" Rodrigo looked surprised. "I did not know 'til I heard him tell his sons." He leaned forward. "Are you really the Gunsmith?"

"I am."

"So," Rodrigo said, "Señor Montoya saved Juanito's life."

"Possibly," Clint said, "or maybe he saved mine."

"Or mine," Rodrigo said.

"So," Clint said, "will they be waiting outside for me?"

"Juanito will want to," Rodrigo said. "He will want to face you alone, and know that he killed the Gunsmith."

"Why don't you do me a favor and go take a look?" Clint said.

"*Sí, señor.*" Rodrigo headed for the door.

"No," Clint said, "don't go to the door. Look out a window."

"Oh, *sí, señor.*"

Rodrigo changed directions and headed for a window. He peered out, taking care not to be seen from outside.

"They are not there, *señor.*"

"What do you think that means?"

Rodrigo turned from the window to look at him.

"Señor Montoya probably would not allow Juanito to wait for you."

"He's a smart man," Clint said. "What would he do?"

"He would probably wait until he had more men before he came after you."

"And why would he come after me?" Clint asked. "We never met until today."

"Well . . . you are the Gunsmith, *señor,*" Rodrigo said. "Is that not enough reason for most men?"

Clint sighed.

"Unfortunately, it is—most of the time."

Clint stood up.

"You are going out there, *señor?*"

"I am."

"But what if they are out there waiting?"

"You just told me you didn't see them."

Rodrigo shrugged.

"What if I simply cannot see them from the window?"

It was Clint's turn to shrug.

"I'll just have to take my chances."

"You can use the back door, *señor*," Carmelita said from the kitchen doorway.

"My horse is out front."

"Rodrigo, he can bring your horse to the back."

"I appreciate the offer," Clint said, "but I'll just go on out the front. How's the hotel?"

"Full of fleas," she said.

He frowned.

"I might have to take my chances with that, too."

"Rodrigo . . ." she said, looking at her husband.

"We have rooms in the back, s*eñor*," he said. "They are not much, but my Carmelita, she keeps them clean."

"How much?"

"Fifty American cents a day."

"Make it a dollar and you have a deal."

Rodrigo smiled and said, "Done, *señor!*"

"I'll have to see to my horse."

"I can take your horse to the livery stable, *señor*," Rodrigo said. "It is owned by my cousin."

"I appreciate the offer, Rodrigo," Clint said, "but I have to go out the front door sometime. It might as well be now."

"Rodrigo—"

Rodrigo spoke quickly to his wife, and she went back into the kitchen.

"What did you tell her?" Clint asked.

"To mind her own business," Rodrigo said.

"Well, I'll go out and get my saddlebags from my horse, and put them in my room. Then I'll take Eclipse—my horse—to your cousin's livery. You wait here."

"*Sí, señor.*"

Clint went to the door, lifted his gun an inch or so to make sure it would slide freely from his holster if he needed it, then dropped it back in and stepped outside.

He stopped just outside the door. Eclipse stared at him, standing right where Clint had left him, with his reins on the ground. He glanced around and saw no sign of Señor Montoya and his two sons. He went to Eclipse and removed his saddlebags, took them back inside.

"Here you go," Clint said, handing them to Rodrigo.

"I will take them to your room, *señor*."

"Which way to your cousin's livery?"

"Go out and to the left, *señor*. At the end of the street, turn left. It is around the corner."

"Okay," Clint said, "I'll be right back."

He went out and followed Rodrigo's directions. He came to a run-down stable, the front doors wide open. Hesitating, he looked around, making sure there were no Montoyas around. Then and only then did he walk to the livery doors. As he stepped inside, he heard a movement to his right.

"I knew you would have to come here, *señor*," Juanito said.

"Does your daddy know you're here?"

"No," Juanito said, "he thinks I am at the trading post. I am here alone, *señor*. For you."

"I just rode into town today," Clint said. "I'm not looking for any trouble."

"You should not have made fun of my name, Señor Adams."

"You're probably right, but I guess it's too late to do anything about that now."

"You must pay the price, *señor*."

"Juanito," Clint said, "this is not a good idea."

"I am a young man, *señor*," Juanito said, "and very good with a pistol. You are old."

"Well," Clint said, "older than you anyway."

FIVE

"Don't push this, Juanito," Clint said. "It won't end well for you."

"You are the one it will not end well for, Señor Gunsmith," Juanito said. "You should not have come to Acuña."

"Do you own this town?" Clint asked.

"My father does."

"Really? He owns the town of Acuña?"

"Everything around it."

"But not the actual town."

Juanito smirked.

"He might as well own it," he said. "The town depends on our money."

"Your money?" Clint asked. "Or your father's?"

"My father's money is also my money."

"I wonder if he thinks the same way."

"It does not matter," Juanito said. "What happens here is only between you and me, señor."

"No," Clint said, "after you force me to kill you, your father and your brother—and probably other family members—will come after me. I will have to kill them, and that will be your fault."

"You will not kill anyone, señor, because you will not

leave this stable alive. And if you do, yes, my family will kill you."

"How many men in your family?"

"My father, my brother, my uncle, and many cousins," Juanito said.

"That figures," Clint said, wishing he had never crossed into Mexico.

Suddenly, another man appeared from inside the stable. He was unarmed, carrying only a bucket.

"Juanito," he said, then asked a question in Spanish. It sounded to Clint like the man was asking what was happening, or what Juanito was doing. The man had to be Rodrigo's cousin, for he was only an inch or so taller than Rodrigo.

Juanito said something to the man, who then stared at Clint.

"*Señor*," he asked, "what is wrong?"

"Juanito is about to do something stupid," Clint said. "Your cousin, Rodrigo, sent me here with my horse, who is outside."

"Why does Juanito want to kill you?"

"Because he's a stupid young man."

The man older than Juanito by some twenty years nodded and said, "*Es verdad, señor.* But if you kill him, you will have to deal with the entire Montoya family."

"Well," Clint said, "the alternative is for me to let him kill me, and I'm not going to do that. If you know this young man, you'd be smart to talk him out of this."

"He is very headstrong, *señor.*"

"That's obvious."

"*Basta!*" Juanito snapped. "Enough. Julio, go away. Do not watch this."

"Julio?" Clint said.

"*Sí?*"

"Is there a lawman in this town?"

"*Sí, señor.* Sheriff Calderon."

"Well," Clint said, "I hope when the time comes, you will tell the sheriff I tried not to kill Juanito."

"Sí, señor."

"Then maybe you should go and see the sheriff, and bring him here."

"Sí, señor," the man said. "I will."

"Go!" Juanito said.

Julio dropped the empty bucket and ran from the livery.

"Enough," Juanito said. "Now you will pay for mocking Juan Hidalgo Montoya de Ramirez, *señor.*"

"Oh, boy," Clint said. "Why do you folks always have such long names?"

Julio ran to the sheriff's office, where he found Sheriff Teodoro Calderon sitting behind his desk, eating greasy chicken with his hands. The portly man had a red-and-white-checked napkin tied around his neck, and was licking grease from his fingers as he looked up at the livery man.

"Julio," he said. *"Que pasa?"*

"You should come quickly to my livery, *Jefe,*" Julio said.

"Why?"

"A gringo is about to kill Juanito Montoya," Julio said anxiously.

"Why?"

"I do not know, *señor.* Perhaps because Juanito is being Juanito," Julio said.

Sheriff Calderon looked down mournfully at the remains of his chicken, then sighed heavily, and removed the napkin from his neck.

"A stupid young boy," he said.

"Sí, señor."

The lawman stood, grabbed his hat and gun belt, and said, *"Andale!"*

SIX

As Sheriff Calderon and Julio approached the livery stable, they heard a shot.

"*Conyo!*" the sheriff swore.

He and Julio ran into the livery, saw Clint Adams standing over Juanito, who was on the ground, his gun still in his holster.

"*Señor!*" Sheriff Calderon yelled, pointing his gun at Clint. "I must ask you for your gun."

Clint looked at the lawman, considering not giving up his gun, but the man looked as if it would only take a small shove to push him over the edge. He did not want to be killed by a nervous lawman.

"I tried not to kill him," Clint said, surrendering his weapon reluctantly. "That should be in my favor."

Calderon looked down at Juanito Montoya, who was rocking back and forth, clutching his bleeding shoulder and not only grimacing in pain, but crying.

"I can see that, *señor*," he said. To Julio, he said, "Go and get the doctor."

"*Sí, Jefe.*"

Calderon leaned over Juanito and said something in Spanish. Clint thought he caught the word "*stupido!*"

The lawman straightened and handed Clint back his pistol.

"What's going on?" Clint asked.

"I will still ask you to accompany me to my office, *señor*," the sheriff said, "but to take your weapon would leave you too defenseless against the Montoyas."

"Are they still in town?"

"That I do not know," the lawman said, "but once they hear that Juanito has been shot, they will be." The sheriff holstered his gun. "I am Sheriff Teodoro Calderon, *señor*."

"Clint Adams."

"Ah," Calderon said, "the Gunsmith. That explains Juanito's stupidity."

"I tried to warn him."

"I am sure you did," Calderon said. "Once the doctor is here, and takes Juanito to his office, we will go to my office and I will take a statement. It will not take long. Where are you staying?"

"At Carmelita's."

"Ah, the back rooms. Well, we will have you there soon enough."

Clint replaced the spent shell in his gun and holstered it.

Once Juanito was carried from the stable by four men, Clint and the sheriff walked to the man's office. Clint told him the whole story, right from the point where the Montoyas entered Carmelita's while he was eating.

"Carmelita's food is the best in town," Sheriff Calderon said.

"So I understand," Clint said. "Do you need anything else from me?"

"No, I think I have enough. I am sure the Montoyas will be here soon."

"What will they do?"

"They will demand that I arrest you."

"And will you?"

"The Montoyas do not tell me how to do my job."

"Juanito told me his father owns the town."

"Everything around the town," the sheriff said, "*sí*, but not the town—and not me."

"That's good to hear."

"Perhaps I will see you at Carmelita's later," Calderon said.

"Perhaps," Clint said.

He left the sheriff's office and walked to Carmelita's Cantina.

"Oh, *señor*," Rodrigo said with relief when he walked in. He put his hand to his heart. "You are all right. We heard the shot and were so worried."

"No, I'm fine."

"And Juanito?"

"Oh, he's still alive," Clint assured him. "He's at the doctor's."

"Then you shot him," Rodrigo said. "But you did not kill him?"

"No," Clint said, "that's why he's at the doctor's. I did not have to kill him. I managed to just shoot him in the shoulder."

Rodrigo looked very concerned nevertheless.

"Señor Montoya, he will still not be happy."

"Maybe he will be," Clint offered, but with little hope. "Maybe he'll be grateful I didn't kill his son. He seemed a sensible man."

"*Sí, señor*," Rodrigo said, "he seemed that way . . . but he is not."

"Well," Clint said, "if anyone is looking for me— Montoya, the sheriff—I'll be in my room."

"I will show you where it is," Rodrigo said. "Come, come . . ."

SEVEN

In the small, clean room, Clint removed his boots and reclined on the bed. In town less than a day and already he had to shoot somebody. Maybe he should not have left the United States. He could have just stayed there and faced the trouble that was already brewing.

But there was no point in thinking that now. It was too late. He was going to have to deal with what had happened. And that meant dealing with the Montoyas.

Unless the elder Montoya—had he heard his first name yet?—actually was a sensible man. He could have let Juanito go ahead and try Clint right there in Carmelita's, backed by himself and his brother. Instead, the boy had snuck away to do it himself. Maybe the father would take some responsibility for that.

Oddly enough, he suddenly found himself hungry. Or was he just yearning for more of Carmelita's food? And a beer?

He pulled his boots on and went out into the hall.

Rodrigo set a mug of beer in front of him while Carmelita made a few tacos. There were also a few other people in the place, eating.

Carmelita brought out a plate of tacos and set it on the bar. Clint was eating his second when the sheriff walked in.

Rodrigo put a beer on the bar for the sheriff, who picked it up quickly.

"*Gracias*," he said. He looked at Clint's platter of tacos. There were four left.

"Do you want one?" Clint asked.

"Very much."

"Go ahead," Clint said, pushing the whole platter toward him. "I only wanted two. I've eaten already."

"*Gracias.*"

Calderon took a taco and bit into it gratefully.

"Did you talk to the Montoyas?"

Calderon swallowed and said, "I did."

"And?"

"The old man was . . . cold. I have never seen him that way before."

"You mean he didn't react?"

"I told him Juanito had been shot and was at the doctor's office."

"And how did he react?"

"That's what worries me," Sheriff Calderon said, snagging another taco. "He didn't react. He just headed for the doctor's office."

"Maybe he's waiting to see what kind of condition his son is in before he decides how to react."

Clint was used to having people "react" to the moment. Montoya seemed to be the kind of man who thought before he reacted.

Clint grabbed another taco even though he'd told the sheriff the rest were his. They were just too good. At that moment Carmelita appeared with another platter and set it on the bar between them. Then she went back into the kitchen. Rodrigo was waiting on the occupied tables.

"Do you think I should go and see Señor Montoya?" Clint asked the lawman.

"No, *señor*, I do not think that would be a good idea," Calderon said. "You should let him come to you, after he has seen Juanito."

"Do you think he'll let this go when he hears what happened?"

"Again, and sadly, no," Calderon said. "For one thing, Juanito will tell him a different story. And there were no witnesses to the shooting, so Señor Montoya will have to decide who to believe, you or his son."

"But he knows the kind of young man his son is."

"*Sí*, he does," the lawman said, "but he is still his son."

"So he'll side with him."

Calderon shrugged.

"That is what family does."

"You know if they come after me, I'll have to defend myself."

"I understand, *señor*."

"And that I can't run?"

"I also understand," Calderon said. "You cannot have the word spread that the Gunsmith ran from a fight."

Rodrigo came back to the bar and gave each man a fresh beer.

"*Gracias, amigo*," Calderon said.

"Do you want to sit?" Rodrigo asked the lawman. "Carmelita can bring out a full meal."

"No, *gracias*," Calderon said. "I must go back to my office. I believe Señor Montoya will be coming back there to make his intentions known." He grabbed two more tacos to take with him. "*Señor*, I would be very, very careful."

"I will," Clint said.

"When I have spoken to Señor Montoya, and I know his intentions, I will let you know."

"Thanks."

Calderon left the cantina and Clint wondered if he was going to be able to trust the man. He was being very helpful to a stranger for some reason.

Why?

EIGHT

Inocencio Montoya entered the doctor's office with his younger son, Pablo, behind him.

"Find the doctor," he said to his son.

"*Sí*, Papa."

Pablo went to a door and opened it, looked inside.

"He is here, Papa, with Juanito."

"Hey!" someone shouted from inside the room. "Shut that door!"

Montoya moved to the doorway, saw the sixtyish sawbones leaning over his boy, who was lying on his back on a table.

"Doctor, I need to speak to my son."

"Well," the doctor said, "I need to tend to this wound, so close that door and I'll be out in a little while."

"Is he all right?" Montoya asked. "Will he live?"

"If you close that door and let me do my job, yes," the doctor said.

Montoya grunted, stepped back, and said to Pablo, "Close the door."

"*Sí*, Papa."

Fifteen minutes later the door reopened and the doctor came out.

"Doctor," Montoya said, "how is he?"

"He has a fairly serious shoulder injury," the doctor said. "I don't think he'll be handling a gun for some time—but he'll live."

"It is the right shoulder?"

"Yes."

"Papa," Pablo said, leaning into his father's ear, "that is his gun—"

"I know that, damn it!" Montoya snapped. "Can I take him home?"

"In a little while, yes," the doctor said. "I'd like him to stay where he is for a while. It was a fairly substantial wound and I wanted to make sure it won't start bleeding again."

"Can I talk to him?"

"Yes, go ahead."

"Pablo," Montoya said, "pay the doctor while I talk to your brother."

"*Sí*, Papa."

Montoya went into the other room. Juanito was still stretched out on the table. He turned his head and looked at his father.

"Papa—"

"*Callate!*" he shouted, telling his son to shut up. "Speak only to answer my questions."

"*Sí*, Papa," Juanito said weakly.

Montoya walked to the table and towered over his son, glaring down at him.

"What did you do?" he demanded. "Idiot!"

"Papa . . . he shot me."

"After you forced him to."

"No—"

"You went after him when I told you not to," Montoya said. "Isn't that right?"

"No, Papa—"

Montoya slapped his son on the head.

"Ow!"

"Do not lie to me!" Montoya growled. "If I am going to be forced to kill this man, I must know the true reason why."

"Papa—"

"Tell me what happened, Juanito," Montoya said. "Everything!"

Juanito sighed and said, "*Sí*, Papa. I went to the livery stable . . ."

Clint remained at the bar, snacking on tacos and beer, while Carmelita and her husband took care of their customers. Some of them were curious about the gringo at the bar; others had heard about the shooting and wondered if he was the man.

He stayed at the bar, expecting the sheriff to come back, or Montoya to show up, but by closing time neither of them had appeared.

Rodrigo locked the front door, then turned to look at Clint.

"Would you like anything else, *señor?*"

"No, Rodrigo," Clint said. "You and Carmelita have done enough. Just finish doing what you have to do each night."

"I must clean up in here while Carmelita cleans the kitchen."

"Can I help?"

"Oh, no, *señor*," Rodrigo said, "you are our guest. Please, just finish your beer—"

"No more beer," Carmelita said, coming out of the kitchen. She was carrying a pot of coffee and a mug.

"Great idea," Clint said happily.

She set the pot and mug on the bar, removed the dregs of his last beer.

"You can drink it here, *señor*, or take it back to your room."

"I'll stay here," he said. "I don't want to make a mess in the room."

"Rodrigo," she shouted, and then went on in Spanish. He

waved with the rag he was using to clean the tables, and she went back into the kitchen.

"What did she say?" Clint asked.

"Oh," Rodrigo said, "she scolded me and told me to make sure I took care of our guest."

"You've both been very hospitable," Clint said. "I appreciate it very much."

"It is an honor to have you here, *señor*," Rodrigo said. "Now, if you will excuse me, I must get a broom."

"Then I think I will take this coffee with me to my room," Clint said. "Good night, Rodrigo."

"See you *mañana, señor.*"

Clint took the pot and the mug and went to his room.

NINE

Inocencio Montoya looked up from his desk at the male members of his family. Spread out in front of him were his son Pablo; his brother, Francisco; his brother's sons, Manuel and Sebastián; the sons of his six sisters; several second and third cousins; as well as some distant relatives.

His older son, Juanito, was up in his room, in bed, sleeping and healing, being tended to by Montoya's wife. The woman was overwrought when they brought her son home, and refused to leave his side.

"You all know what has happened."

"*Sí*, the gringo, Clint Adams, shot Juanito," Pablo said.

Montoya glared at his son, who subsided.

"Juanito was foolish enough to face the Gunsmith in a gunfight. He was an idiot! And he was shot. He is lucky he was not killed. The gringo could have killed him easily, if he wanted to. I must give the gringo my gratitude for that . . . just before I kill him."

"Papa?"

"He shot Juanito," Montoya said. "Whatever the reason was, he must pay."

"With his life, Inocencio?" Francisco asked, looking doubtful.

"But with what else, my brother?" Montoya said. "How else would he pay?"

No one had an answer. None of them wanted to contradict the head of the family.

"We will all back you, my brother," Francisco assured him. "When will we do it?"

Montoya sat back in his chair and sighed.

"I will talk to the gringo, and then make my decision," he said. "That is all. I will say good night to you now."

Slowly, the men all began to file from the room. At the end, only Pablo and Francisco remained.

"Pablo," Montoya said. "Go to bed."

"But Papa—"

"Go!"

Slowly, reluctantly, Pablo left the room. That left Inocencio alone with his brother.

"Is this a wise decision, Inocencio?" Francisco asked.

"What would you have me do?" Montoya asked. "What would you do if it was one of your sons?"

"My sons are neither so foolhardy nor so brave as Juanito."

"Brave," Montoya said, "yes, he is brave . . . too brave for his own good. But still . . . if it was your son, would you let it be?"

Francisco, several years younger than the sixty-year-old Montoya, still had dark hair and beard, while his brother had gone gray many years ago. Perhaps it was the difference in their sons that had driven him gray.

"I suppose I would do the same thing," he said finally. "But you cannot do it alone."

"I am not so foolish to think I can stand against a man like the Gunsmith alone," Montoya said. "That is why I gathered the entire family."

"I do not think you should even go and speak with him alone," Francisco said. "I will go with you."

Montoya smiled at his brother.

"You think your cooler head will keep me from doing something foolish?"

Now it was Francisco's turn to smile.

"Perhaps you are right," Montoya said. "Very well, then. We will go and see the Gunsmith together."

"When?"

"Tomorrow morning," Montoya said.

"Do we have breakfast first?"

Montoya smiled at that.

"We will have breakfast with the Gunsmith," he said. "At Carmelita's."

TEN

Clint woke up in the morning with no direct sunlight coming through the tiny window. His room was in the rear of the building, facing west. Still, his instincts told him it was time for breakfast. That and his stomach.

He used the pitcher-and-basin Rodrigo had supplied him with to wash up, dressed, and went down the hall into the cantina.

There were already customers in Carmelita's for breakfast. Clint was happy to see that. He was concerned that they didn't do enough business. Apparently, breakfast was a busy time for them.

The four tables were occupied, so he went to the bar.

"Ah, good morning, *señor*," Rodrigo said. "Did you sleep well?"

"Very well, Rodrigo, thanks."

"Do you want some coffee while you wait for a table?" Rodrigo asked.

"I don't need a table, Rodrigo," Clint said. "I'll eat right here."

"What would you like, *señor*?"

"Whatever you want to bring me, I'll eat," Clint said.

Rodrigo smiled and said, "I will tell Carmelita to make

something special. Start with this." He poured Clint a mug of strong black coffee.

"*Gracias*," Clint said.

Rodrigo went into the kitchen, came out with both arms loaded with plates, which he distributed around the room.

On his next trip to and from the kitchen, he brought out a huge platter of breakfast burritos for Clint and set them down on the bar.

"*Dar gusto!*" he said.

"*Gracias*," Clint said again, and dug in.

He watched as people ate with enjoyment, left, and gave their tables up to more people who ate that way. Everyone smiled and greeted Rodrigo like a friend, and he treated them the same way.

Clint was halfway through his platter of burritos when two men entered the cantina, and all conversation stopped. Rodrigo turned and stared at the doorway, his eyes widening.

"Why do you look so surprised, Rodrigo?" Inocencio Montoya said.

"Señor Montoya," he said. "I—I did not expect to see you."

"Are my brother and I not welcome as customers in your establishment?"

"No, no, of course you are welcome," Rodrigo said.

Clint thought this conversation was being held in English for his benefit.

"I will get you a table—"

"No need," Montoya said. "My brother and I will eat at the bar, alongside Señor Adams."

The two men strolled to the bar and stood next to Clint, who was encouraged that they had not flanked him.

"Señor Adams, you remember me?" Montoya asked.

"Of course I do, Señor Montoya," he said.

"This is my younger brother, Francisco."

"*Señor*," Clint said.

Francisco Montoya nodded.

"Rodrigo," Montoya said, "we will have what the *señor* is having. It looks delicious."

"*Sí, señor*," Rodrigo said, "I will tell my wife."

Before he went to the kitchen, however, he poured them each a cup of coffee.

"Señor Montoya," Clint said, "allow me to tell you how much I regret what happened between your son and me yesterday. I'm afraid he gave me no choice."

"I am sure he did not, *señor*," Montoya said. "I must thank you for not killing him. It would probably have been easy for you. Juanito fancies himself a . . . a *pistolero* . . . but he is no match for you."

"I was happy I could avoid it," Clint said, wondering where this conversation was heading.

The two men drank their coffee, and when Rodrigo appeared quickly with a platter of breakfast burritos, they began to eat with great gusto. But Clint was sure they had not come for his apology, or to express gratitude and have breakfast with him. Something else was coming.

"How is your son, by the way?" Clint asked.

"He is recovering," Montoya said. "His mother is tending to him. I have to tell you, she wants very much for me to kill you."

"Well . . ." Clint said. "She is his mother, after all."

"I am glad you understand," Montoya said.

"Of course I do—"

"Then you will understand that, as his father, I also want to kill you," Montoya said. "In fact, I intend to kill you."

Clint sipped his coffee and tried to appear nonchalant.

"Is that what you came here to do?" he asked. "Warn me?"

"No, no, *señor*," Montoya said. "I am not warning you. I am expressing to you a fact. For shooting my son Juanito, I will kill you. I *must*."

ELEVEN

"Oh," Montoya went on, "not here, not now. Enjoy your breakfast, please . . . but soon."

"Do you mind if I ask why?" Clint asked. "You know he gave me no choice."

"I understand," Montoya said. "He was headstrong, stupid even. But he is still my son. And I have a reputation to protect, as you do."

"I don't care about my reputation."

"But of course you do," Montoya said. "If you were to run from a fight with someone like my son, that would not have been good for your reputation. Others would come looking for you."

"They come looking anyway."

"But they would come in droves, *señor!*" Montoya said. "No, no, you could not afford that. Just as I cannot afford to just let you leave town after shooting my son. Do you understand?"

"I'm afraid I do, *señor.*"

"Ah, good, good," Montoya said. "Then you must also understand that I am not as foolish as my son. I will not come after you alone."

"I didn't think you would," Clint said, looking past Montoya at Francisco.

"Oh, with my brother, yes," Montoya said, "but also with the rest of my family. You see, there is the family honor to uphold."

"I see."

"And please understand," Montoya said, "I am not happy about this. This gives me no joy. I am very upset with my son for putting me in this position."

"No doubt."

"You are a very understanding man, *señor*."

"Well," Clint said, "we are grown men, are we not?"

"*Sí, sí*," Montoya said, "we are grown men."

"So then you'll understand when I give you a warning," Clint said.

"*Señor?*"

"If you come after me with your whole family, I will not be as understanding as I was with your son," Clint said. "I will have to kill to protect myself."

"*Sí, sí*," Montoya said, "I understand this."

"Does he understand it?" Clint asked, indicating Montoya's brother. "I'll have to kill you, your other son, him, and his sons."

"All of us, *señor?*" Montoya asked doubtfully. "Really?"

"As many as I can take with me." He put down his coffee cup and stepped closer to the man. "Starting with you."

They stared at each other for a long moment, and then Montoya stepped back and raised his hands.

"But not now, *señor*," he said, "for as you see, I came in here unarmed."

"So you did," Clint said, also stepping back. He picked up a burrito with his left hand.

"Please, gentlemen," Rodrigo said, "there will be no gunplay in my establishment."

"No, Rodrigo," Clint said, "there won't be. Señor Montoya was very smart to come in unarmed."

"You will find, *señor*," Montoya said, "that I am always very smart in my approach to . . . everything." He put down his coffee cup, wiped his hands on his shirt. "Enjoy the rest of your breakfast."

He turned and went out, followed closely by his brother who, Clint noticed, had never quite been able to look him in the eye.

Outside, Francisco grabbed his brother's arm when they reached their horses. Montoya turned to look at him, saw how pale he was.

"I thought he was going to kill us."

"No, no," Montoya said, putting his hand on his brother's shoulder, "that is why I had us go in unarmed, so there would be no danger of that."

"But . . . how did you know he would not?"

"He did not kill Juanito when he had the chance," Montoya explained.

"No, he did not."

"He does not want to kill."

"But . . . he is the Gunsmith."

"You cannot always believe a man's reputation, Francisco," Montoya said, retrieving his gun from his horse and sticking it into his belt.

"Should we wait for him here, then?" Francisco said, retrieving his own weapon.

"No," Montoya said. "I meant what I said, Cisco. We will come for him with the whole family."

"But . . . he will kill someone."

Montoya placed his hand on his brother's shoulder once again and said, "Perhaps he will only kill a second cousin or two, eh?"

TWELVE

After the Montoya brothers left the cantina, Rodrigo heaved a sigh of relief.

"*Señor,*" he said to Clint, "I was very frightened."

"I won't allow gunplay in your place, my friend," Clint assured him.

"*Gracias, señor.*"

Clint looked around, saw the other diners staring at him.

"Tell your customers they can go back to eating," he said. "The excitement is over."

"*Sí, señor.*"

Rodrigo came around from behind the bar and went to each table to relay that information.

Clint poured himself some more coffee, and contemplated the situation as he looked at the unfinished burritos before him. He understood Montoya perfectly. There was no way the man could simply allow him to leave town. He would lose face. That was very important to a prideful Mexican like Inocencio Montoya. Besides, he had the boy's mother to answer to.

It looked like he had two choices—stay and fight, or leave. He had gone against his better judgment already when he left Texas ahead of the possibility of trouble. This time, however, the trouble was obvious, and to leave town would mean being perceived as having run from it.

On the other hand, how smart was it to stand and fight when you were outnumbered by . . .

"Rodrigo?" he asked as the man came back behind the small bar.

"Sí, señor?"

"How many men are in the Montoya family?"

"Oh . . . many, *señor.* There are many cousins . . ."

"How many sons does Montoya have?"

"Just the two you have already seen."

"And how many brothers does he have?"

"One," Rodrigo said, "just Francisco."

"And many sons does he have?"

"Two."

"And how many cousins?"

"Well," Rodrigo said, "there are second cousins, and third cousins . . ."

"Do you know how many?"

"Sadly, I do not."

"Okay, thank you."

So he knew of five Montoyas who might be coming for him. He needed to know more, however, and there was only one man he could think of to ask.

He went to his room to fetch his hat . . .

Clint found the sheriff's office in a small adobe building with a thick, heavy oak door. He knocked and entered.

The inside was cramped, and he found himself only about three feet from Sheriff Calderon, seated at his desk.

"Ah, buenos dias, señor!" the man said.

"Not a very big office, is it?" Clint asked.

"I have one cell in the back," Calderon said, "but I rarely need it."

"Deputies?"

Calderon threw his arms out to his sides and said, "Alas, just me."

Clint looked around, saw a small wooden chair against the wall.

"May I sit?"

"Please."

He pulled the chair over and sat.

"I cannot offer you any coffee," the man said. "There is no room in here for a coffeepot."

"And no stove, I notice. How do you stay warm when it's cold?"

"Many blankets, but I do not complain," the portly Calderon said. "So what can I do for you on this beautiful day, eh, *señor?*"

"Señor Montoya came to Carmelita's this morning and announced, in front of witnesses, his intention to kill me," Clint explained.

Calderon frowned.

"I was afraid of that."

"Actually," Clint said, "he announced that it was his family's intention to kill me."

"They are a very close family, *señor,*" Calderon said. "They will obey the patriarch."

"Well, my question for you is," Clint said, "how many of them will I have to face? He came in with his brother, so I assume with them and their sons—and with Juanito out of commission—there would be five."

"*Sí, señor.*"

"But I understand there are cousins?"

"Many cousins."

"But Montoya has only one brother."

"*Si, señor,*" Calderon said, "but he also has six sisters, and they all have children."

"All boys?"

"Oh, no, *señor,*" Calderon said, "there are some girls."

"That's a relief."

"But not many."

"Oh."

"Did Señor Montoya say when this event would take place?" Calderon asked.

"He did not."

"*Señor*," Calderon said, "I would suggest that you leave town."

"First of all," Clint said, "would that end it? Would he let me go?"

"No," Calderon said, "he would come after you."

"Into Texas?"

"Oh, *sí*, anywhere."

"Then what's the point of leaving?"

"*Señor*, in Texas perhaps you can find someone to help you," Calderon said. "I assume you have many friends who live by their gun?"

"I do," Clint said, "but they all have their own problems. If I stay, how many members of the Montoya family do you think I will have to face?"

"Oh . . ." Calderon did some sums in his head before answering. "*Señor*, I would say . . . at least twenty easily."

"I was afraid you'd say something like that."

THIRTEEN

"So what will you do, *señor?*"

"I think," Clint said thoughtfully, "perhaps I'll start drinking early today."

Teodoro Calderon exploded out of his seat and exclaimed excitedly, "An excellent idea, *señor.* And I think I will join you."

"But not at Carmelita's," Clint said.

"I know just the place." The lawman grabbed his hat, took his pistol from his desk, and tucked it in his belt. "I will show you."

Sheriff Calderon led Clint down the street to a small cantina that did not serve food, only beer and whiskey.

"Is this what you had in mind, *señor?*" Calderon asked.

"This is exactly what I had in mind."

They went to the bar, where a bored-looking bartender in his fifties was serving several Mexicans. He finished and looked over at them.

"Ah, *Jefe,*" he said. "A little early, is it not?"

"My *amigo* needs a drink, Jorge," Calderon said, "and I cannot allow him to drink alone."

"Then what will you and your *amigo* have?"

"*Cerveza*," Clint said, "and a shot of whiskey."

"The same, Jorge," Calderon said.

"Excellent choice."

There were several other men in the place, all Mexican, all drinking early. They looked over at Clint and the sheriff, but did not seem particularly interested in them.

The bartender set up their beer and whiskey, and went to the other end of the bar. Clint picked up the shot of whiskey and tossed it down. The sheriff followed.

"Another?" Calderon asked.

"One's enough." Clint picked up his beer and took a swallow. "Tell me something."

"If I can," Calderon said.

"What will you do after they kill me?"

"I will have to investigate the matter to see if there was any wrongdoing."

Clint looked at the lawman.

"Twenty men kill one and you won't know if there is any wrongdoing until you investigate?"

"It is my job," Calderon said. "I cannot jump to any conclusions."

"What if I kill Señor Montoya, and his brother, and his sons, and the cousins decide to leave me alone? What then?"

"Again," the sheriff said, "I will have to look into the matter."

"I'm pretty sure it will be a matter of self-defense."

"Ah, but once again," Calderon said, "I cannot leap to any conclusions."

"What about backing me?" Clint asked. "Backing my play?"

"I am afraid I would not be able to take sides."

If Sheriff Calderon was not in Montoya's pocket, he was doing a pretty good impression of it.

"What about others?"

"What others?"

"Other men in town who might back my play?" Clint said.

"Would you pay them?"

"I would."

The sheriff thought a moment.

"You speak of mercenaries."

"If that's what it takes."

"I doubt there are men in town who would go against Montoya," Calderon said, "but there may be some—other gringos—who might, for the right price."

"Where would I find them?"

"I think I can tell you."

FOURTEEN

Sheriff Calderon gave Clint three names, all gringos, men who sold their guns separately, but may have worked together a time or two.

"Two live on this side of the border, one just over the border in Texas," the lawman said, "but they all ply their trade here."

"Will they go against the Montoyas?"

"For the right price."

"Have they ever worked for Montoya?"

"Perhaps."

"All right." Clint finished his beer and set the empty mug down. "I guess I better have a talk with them. Is there a telegraph office in town?"

"No, *señor.*"

"One near here?"

"In Texas," the man said, "many miles from here."

Clint was thinking of sending word for help to some of his friends, but if it was too far to go to send telegrams, that didn't seem to be an option.

So for now, the option seemed to be mercenaries.

"Thanks for your help, Sheriff," Clint said.

"I hope you find more help than I have been able to give you, *señor.*"

Clint left Calderon in the cantina, ordering another beer.

The first man's name was Willie Piper. He lived in an abandoned house on the outskirts of Acuña. According to Calderon, he was an ex-Army man who was proficient with many weapons. He was a deserter who had come to Mexico to escape prosecution.

Clint probably could have walked to the house, but he decided to ride Eclipse, just in case the Montoyas made a try for him.

He got within a hundred feet of the run-down adobe house when there was a shot, and a bullet kicked up some dirt in front of him. Eclipse shied only slightly.

"Stop right there!" a voice called.

"I'm looking for Willie Piper!"

"What for?"

"I want to hire him."

"For how much?"

"A lot of money."

There was silence, then the voice said, "Come ahead."

Clint rode up to the house and stopped.

"Step down."

He did.

"Drop your gun," the voice said from inside.

"Can't do that."

"I've got a gun on you."

"I figured."

"So drop yours."

"Can't."

Dead silence, then the voice asked curiously, "Who are you?"

"My name's Clint Adams."

"The Gunsmith?"

"That's right."

The door to the house opened and a man stepped out. He was wearing an old Army uniform with the insignia removed. He was tall, rangy, hard-looking, white-haired, in his fifties. His face bore the scars of years as a soldier. He was holding a shotgun.

"Clint Adams," he said. "Really?"

"That's right."

He squinted against the sunlight.

"You down here on a bounty?"

"I'm not a bounty hunter."

"Somebody send you after me?"

"Nope," Clint said. "You think you're still wanted in the States?"

Piper shrugged. "There's no limit on desertion."

"Why'd you desert?"

"I got tired of it," Piper said.

"The fighting?"

"The orders." The man grinned. "I like fighting."

"That's what I was hoping you'd say."

The man squinted at him, lowered the shotgun slightly.

"You really lookin' to hire me?"

"I am."

"For a lot of money?"

"That's right."

Piper lowered the shotgun the rest of the way, held it down by his leg.

"Come on in."

"Don't you want to know what the job is first?"

"You said the magic word."

"What's that?"

"Money." Piper stepped aside. "Come on in and tell me the rest."

FIFTEEEN

Piper had the bare essentials in the house. A cot, a table, two chairs, a working stove. And weapons. Hanging on pegs on the wall were a variety of rifles and shotguns.

"Drink?"

"Why not?"

"Have a seat."

Clint pulled a chair out and sat at the table. Piper put the shotgun down, but Clint saw that he had a gun tucked into his belt. The man grabbed two tin cups and a bottle of whiskey from the stove counter and carried them to the table. He poured two drinks, and sat opposite Clint.

"What's on your mind?"

"You know the Montoyas?"

"Inocencio Montoya?"

"That's right."

"I know him."

"Ever work for him?"

"No. You havin' trouble with the Montoyas?"

"I am," Clint said. "I shot his son Juanito."

"Oh, boy," Piper said. "Kill 'im?"

"No," Clint said, "I shot him in the shoulder."

Piper frowned.

"Is that what you meant to do?"

"Yes," Clint said, "I didn't want to kill him."

"And I guess Señor Montoya isn't showing you the proper gratitude?"

"He actually came to me and told me he appreciated it," Clint said, "but he also told me he had to kill me to save face."

"Don't you think you can handle the old fella?" Piper asked.

"The old fella has some help," Clint said. "His whole family."

"Wait," Piper said. "His whole Mexican family?"

"That's right."

"Whew," Piper said, "that means second and third cousins, probably even godsons."

"You can see my problem."

"Yeah," Piper said, "but you seem to have a fast horse out there."

"Running is not an option. It wouldn't look good for me."

"I can see that," Piper said, "but what do you want me to do, stand with you against twenty or thirty angry Mexicans?"

"I was thinking . . ."

"You got enough money to make me even consider that?" Piper asked, pouring himself some more whiskey.

"A thousand dollars?"

Piper stopped with his cup halfway to his lips, then lowered it and peered across the table at Clint. He had at least a week's worth of stubble on his chin.

"You got a thousand dollars?"

"Yes."

"On you?"

"No."

"Where then? Your hotel?"

"I'll get it from a bank."

"There ain't no bank in Acuña."

"I'll go to the nearest bank and get the money," Clint said.

"Nearest bank's fifty miles away," Piper said. "You head for that bank, Montoya will think you're running."

"Well," Clint said, "I could pay you after the job is done."

"And if we're both dead after the job is done?"

"Then you wouldn't be able to spend the money anyway."

Piper stared at him a few moments, then let out a bark of laughter and said, "You're right about that. And this would be a chance for me to stand with the Gunsmith."

"Against insurmountable odds," Clint said, raising his cup. "You got anything else to do right now?"

"Nope," Piper said, "but if we do come out of this alive, I can count on you to pay me?"

"I'm a man of my word."

"I ain't never heard anybody say different about you," Piper had to admit.

They clinked cups and drank.

"So," Piper said, "just the two of us against the Montoyas?"

"I heard some talk about two more men in the area who might join us."

"That so? Who?"

"Jed Autry and Mel Harker. You know them?"

"I know Jed," Piper said. "He's been down here almost as long as I have."

"Will he do it for a thousand?"

"He'd do it for a hundred," Piper said, "but don't tell him I said that."

"I'll pay him the same as I pay you," Clint said. "What about Harker?"

"Heard of him," Piper said, "but I don't know him. He lives over the border, though."

"I'll risk it," Clint said.

"It ain't so far that Montoya will think you're runnin',"

Piper said. "If you want, I can go with ya to talk to both of them."

"You think I'll need your help to talk them into it?" Clint asked.

Piper drained his cup and said, "I think it'll help if they see you got somebody with ya who's as crazy as you are."

SIXTEEN

They decided to go and see Jed Autry first. He lived closer, already being in Mexico.

Piper saddled up his horse, an eight-year-old Indian pony with spotted haunches.

He led Clint to a freestanding building, nothing else around it. There were some horses outside, and behind it a small stable.

"If this is a town," Clint said, "it's a lot smaller than Acuña."

"Not a town," Piper said.

"He lives here?"

"He doesn't live here, but it's the place where you'll find Jed Autry—a cathouse."

Inside, Jed Autry was in room six with a girl named Ginger. She was a tall, lean redhead, complete with freckles, green eyes, and a burnished copper bush.

At the moment she was reclining naked on her bed, her hands above her head, drawing her small breasts taut. If Autry could have seen them, he would have loved them, but at the moment his face was between her legs, and his nose was buried in that copper bush.

"Oh, honey, yeah," she moaned as he probed her with his tongue. "Where did you learn this? Mmm, the men around here just don't do that!"

Most of the men who came to the cathouse were Mexican, and except for Ginger and a blond *gringa* named Jenny, the other girls were all Mexican. But every so often a gringo came over the border, and yet no one except Autry had done this to her.

She brought her hands down to cup the back of his head, and press him even more firmly into her. Autry moaned, enjoying the tastes of her, as well as the scratchy feel of the pubic hair on his cheeks.

That's when there was a knock on the door . . .

"He's upstairs with Ginger," Madam Rosa said. "He won't like being interrupted."

"Tell him," Piper said, "there's a man down here who wants to pay him a thousand dollars."

Rosa's eyebrows went up and she asked, "One of you has a thousand dollars on you?"

Clint looked at the short, stout, plump, middle-aged madam and said, "No, not on me. Just tell him."

"I will send Hernando up to tell him."

Clint didn't know who Hernando was, but he assumed he was some sort of handyman in the cathouse. She left the foyer, and moments later a thin young man bounded up the stairs to the second floor.

"Goddamnit!" Autry shouted.

"Oh God, honey, don't stop!" Ginger exclaimed. "You can't stop now!"

"I can't concentrate!" he yelled.

He bounced off the bed and ran to the door, naked. He was prepared to smash whoever was standing in the hall. When he opened the door, Hernando cringed at the big man—and at his huge cock, which somehow seemed to be pointing at him accusingly.

"What the hell—" Autry shouted.

"*Señor*, I am sorry," Hernando said, "I have a message for you."

"What?"

"I don't know," Hernando said. "Madam Rosa told me to tell you there's a man downstairs who wants to give you a thousand dollars."

"Dollars?" Autry said. "American dollars?"

"*Sí, señor.*"

"A thousand?"

"*Sí, señor.*"

"What man?"

"I do not know, *señor*. There are two men, both gringos. One has white hair."

"White?" Autry thought immediately of Willie Piper, so the man with the money had to be the other one.

"Okay, tell them I'll be down."

"*Sí, señor.*" The young man turned and fled gratefully down the hall.

Autry slammed the door and turned to the naked girl on the bed.

"You can't leave me like this!" she moaned.

"I hate to do it, babe," he said, grabbing his clothes, "but do you have a thousand and one dollars for me?"

"No, damnit!"

She watched his impressive erection disappear inside his pants. She hadn't even spent any time with it.

"Come back when you're finished," she called as he went out the door.

"If I can, babe," he said, "but I can't make any promises."

SEVENTEEN

Clint was impressed by the sheer size of the man who came down the stairs. He had to be six foot six, with broad shoulders and—judging from the fit of his clothes—not an ounce of fat on him. He was buttoning his shirt over a huge hairy chest, and had his gun belt slung over his shoulder.

"Piper!" he boomed. "What the fuck?"

"Sorry to interrupt you, Jed," Piper said, "but I got a man here with money burning a hole in his pocket."

"That little greaser said something about a thousand dollars."

"That's the price," Clint said.

"To do what?" Autry demanded.

"Is there somewhere we can sit so I can explain?" Clint asked.

"Rosa!"

"*Sí, señor?*" she replied meekly from behind him.

"Clear the parlor, and bring us some whiskey."

She sighed and said, "*Sí, señor.*"

She went into the parlor ahead of them, and suddenly a bunch of scantily clad women—most Mexican, one blond—came scurrying out.

"In here!" Autry said.

Clint and Piper followed him into the now empty parlor.
Madam Rosa appeared with a tray holding three shots of
whiskey, then withdrew.

"You own the place?" Clint asked.

"Let's just say I'm an investor," Autry said. "Have a seat."

Clint and Piper each took a sofa. Jed Autry seemed to
fill the whole room with his bulk. Clint figured the man
would be good to have on your side in a close-up fight, but
he didn't know how he'd be with a gun.

"What's this about?" Autry asked. "A thousand dollars?"

"You know Inocencio Montoya?" Clint asked.

"Yeah," Autry said, "I've heard of him."

"Ever work for him?"

"Nope." He sipped his whiskey. "Wait. You goin' after
Montoya?"

"The opposite," Clint said. "They're coming after me."

"They?"

"The whole family."

"Whoa," Autry said. "You got trouble."

"That's why I'm here."

Jed Autry looked over at Piper. "So what's your part in
this?"

"A thousand dollars."

"That's it?"

"No," Piper said, jerking his head toward Clint. "He's
Clint Adams."

"The Gunsmith?" Autry looked surprised.

"A chance to stand with the Gunsmith," Piper said.

"Against insurmountable odds," Clint added.

"Are there any other kind?" Autry asked with a grin.
"Sounds like fun."

Autry got his horse from in front of the whorehouse, and
the three of them rode off.

"You give him my name?" Autry asked Piper.

"Uh-uh," Piper said. "He already had yours, mine, and Mel Harker's."

"Harker," Autry said. "He's in Texas."

"That's where we're goin'."

Clint turned in his saddle to look back at them.

"Is that a problem?"

"Texas?" Autry asked. "Not for me. But Harker?"

"What about him?"

"We've butted heads a time or two."

"Really?" Clint asked. "He come out the worse for it?"

"Let's just say Harker gives as good as he gets," Autry said with a grin.

"What about you?" Clint asked Piper. "You got a problem going to Texas?"

"It's only a few miles," Piper said. "Should be okay."

"All right, then," Clint said. "Somebody lead the way."

EIGHTEEN

Just across the Mexico-Texas border was a town called Del Rio. As the three men crossed the Rio Grande, Clint thought—as he had thought many times before—that the air just felt different when you got back to the U.S. side.

"You feel it, too, huh?" Piper asked him.

Clint looked at him, and nodded. "I thought I was the only one."

"Naw," Piper said. "I feel it every time."

"You miss it?"

Piper shook his head.

"I been away too long," he said. "It ain't home to me anymore."

"I guess I can understand that."

Autry was riding on ahead, and came back to them now.

"The house is just over the rise," he said.

"He doesn't live in town?" Clint asked.

"No," Autry said, "he couldn't live in a town any more than me or Piper could."

Clint looked at Piper.

"It's true," the man said. "Too damn many people."

"Can't stand crowds anymore," Autry said, then grinned and added, "unless they're women."

"Okay," Clint said, "lead the way to his house, then."

"He's bound to shoot at us as we approach," Autry said.

"Then let's hope he misses," Clint said.

Riding a ways behind them was a man named José Perez. He worked for Inocencio Montoya, not as a gunman but as a *vaquero*. Still, from time to time the *patrón* gave him a special job to do . . . like this one.

"I want you to watch the gringo, Clint Adams."

José swallowed and asked, "The Gunsmith, *patrón?*"

"That's right, the Gunsmith," Montoya said. "I do not wish for you to engage him, just watch him, and let me know if he leaves Mexico. Not if he just goes over the border, but if he is leaving—running from me. *Comprende?*"

"*Sí*, I understand, *patrón.*"

"Then go."

"*Patrón*—what if he sees me?"

"I expect him to see you, José," Montoya said, "but do not worry. He will not do anything to you."

"He won't?"

"Do you trust me, José?"

"*Sí, patrón*, I trust you."

"Then go and do my bidding," Montoya said, "and I will see to it that you receive a bonus."

José Perez swallowed hard and said, "*Sí, patrón.* I will do as you ask."

"*Bueno*, José," Montoya said to the young man, "*muy bueno.*"

After José left the house, Montoya's wife, Maria, came down the stairs. She glared at him with fire in her eyes.

"How is he?" he asked.

"He is in pain," she said. "How do you think he is?"

In her fifties, after having two sons, she was still a beautiful woman.

"When will you make this gringo pay for what he did?"

"Soon, *querida*," he said, "very soon. Do not worry. I have it all planned."

And Clint did see the man.

So did Piper and Autry.

"You want me to ride back and get rid of him?" Autry asked.

"Kill him?" Clint asked.

"Naw," Autry said, "just cripple him a bit so he can't follow us."

"No," Clint said, "let him follow. He's just keeping an eye on me for his boss."

"You don't mind?" Piper asked.

"Montoya just wants to be sure I don't run."

"And if you did?" Autry asked.

"He'd come after me," Clint said, "with his whole family."

"Even over the border?" Piper asked.

"To the ends of the earth," Clint said.

The house was quite a bit different from the one Clint had found Piper in. This one had been kept up well, had a corral adjacent to it with a few horses in it, a small barn next to that.

"Looks like this might be a working horse ranch," Clint commented.

"He tries," Autry said, "but he takes jobs across the border to make ends meet."

"He doesn't work on this side of the border?"

"He tries not to break the law in Texas, or the U.S. for that matter."

Clint wondered what Autry's background was. The big man sounded educated most of the time. Piper, on the other hand, sounded trail educated.

As they approached the house, there was a shot. Hot lead kicked up some dirt in front of them. Eclipse simply stopped, while Piper's and Autry's mounts shied and had to be steadied.

"Harker, damn it!" Autry shouted. "It's me, Jed Autry."

"Oh yeah?" Harker asked. "Who's that with ya?"

"Willie Piper and Clint Adams!"

Harker hesitated, then yelled, "Clint Adams? You mean the Gunsmith?"

"That's right."

"What's he want?"

"He wants to give you some money."

There was some more silence, and then Harker shouted, "Okay, come ahead."

As they rode up to the house, the front door opened and a stocky man in his forties stepped out, carrying a rifle.

"That's far enough," he said. "Piper I know on sight, so I guess you'd be Adams."

"That's right."

"What's this about money? How much we talkin' about?"

"Actually," Clint said, "it's a job—"

"Well, of course it's a job, ya damned fool," Harker said. "I didn't think you just wanted to gimme some money. How much are we talkin'?"

"Don't you want to know what the job is?"

"Well, you got these two with ya, so I guess it's got to do with gunplay. I ain't gonna ask ya again. How much?"

"A thousand dollars."

Harker blinked.

"You got it on ya?"

"No," Clint said, "I'll have to get it from a bank after the job is done."

"You're gonna borrow from a bank to pay us?"

"Not borrow," Clint said, "withdraw. The money is already in there."

"Where'd you get that kinda money?"

"Does it matter?" When Harker didn't answer, Clint added, "I won it playing poker."

Harker squinted up at Clint, much the same way Piper

had done earlier in the day, then said, "Ya might as well step down. Sounds like we got some things to talk about."

The three men stepped down, secured their horses—Clint dropped Eclipse's reins to the ground—then followed Harker into the house.

All of the furniture in the house—table, a desk, a sofa, and chairs—looked handmade.

"You do all this yourself?" Clint asked.

"I did. I do my work out back."

"It's all nice work," Clint said.

Grudgingly, Harker said, "Thanks." He hung his rifle on two hooks on the wall and asked, "Y'all want some coffee?"

They all nodded, and Clint said, "Sure."

"Sit at the table," Harker said.

They all took chairs at the table. Harker brought coffee and sat in the fourth chair.

"What's it about?"

Clint gave Harker the same explanation he'd given to Piper and Autry.

"I worked for Montoya," he said when Clint was done. "He's not a man you want to go against."

"He's not giving me much of a choice."

"We all got choices," Harker said. He looked at Piper and Autry. "Y'all in on this?"

"I can use the money," Piper said.

"A thousand dollars is a thousand dollars," Autry said.

Harker looked at Clint again, but spoke to the others. "Is he gonna pay?"

"Oh, he'll pay," Piper said.

"If we come out of it alive," Autry added.

NINETEEN

Clint, Piper, and Autry rode back across the border to Texas. Harker told them he'd join them by that night.

"Just gotta get my neighbor to watch my place," he said, "and take care of my horses."

He walked them outside, and as Clint mounted up, the man asked, "You wouldn't be interested in selling that horse, would you?"

"Not a chance," Clint said.

"I'll make you a good price."

"Not at any price," Clint told him.

"Can't say I blame you," Harker admitted.

They arranged to meet in Acuña, at Carmelita's, by nightfall.

When they got near Acuña, Clint suggested that Piper and Autry both go to Piper's house and wait there until dark.

"Why?" Piper asked. "Our tail will tell Montoya about the three of us as soon as he gets back to the Montoya ranch."

Clint looked behind them. The rider could no longer be seen. He assumed that once they rode back into Mexico and headed for Acuña, he must have peeled off and returned to the ranch.

"Just the same," Clint said, "let's keep some space between us until we meet at Carmelita's."

Piper looked at Autry, who shrugged and said, "Clint's the boss."

They agreed, and split up from that point.

José Perez entered the Montoya house and waited just inside the front door.

"José," Montoya said, coming down the stairs from the second floor.

"Patrón."

"What do you have for me?"

Briefly, José outlined everything he had seen Clint Adams do since that morning. Montoya listened intently, nodding from time to time, but never interrupting.

"And where are they now?"

"Back in Mexico, *patrón*," José said. "I think they are going back to Acuña."

"All of them?"

"Well . . . they were all riding that way."

Montoya frowned.

"José, you disappoint me."

"But *patrón*, I have brought you all this information," José said.

"But you can't tell me where these four men are right now," Montoya pointed out.

"Señor—"

"Never mind," Montoya said. "I obviously trusted the wrong man with this job."

"Patrón . . . am I fired?"

"No, you are not fired," Montoya said, "but you will receive no bonus. Go back to work."

"Sí, patrón."

José left the room and Montoya walked into the living room, where he also had his desk in front of the large front window. He poured himself a glass of tequila and took it to his desk.

Actually, José had not disappointed him terribly. He now knew that Clint Adams had three men backing his play, three mercenaries Montoya had heard of, one of whom he had even employed himself. But he knew the reputations of all three. They were fighting men.

He looked up as his brother, Francisco, entered the room.

"We will be eating soon," he said.

"Have a drink, brother," Montoya said. "I have some news."

Francisco poured himself a drink and sat down across from his brother. Montoya told him what he had learned.

"We can probably buy Harker," Francisco said. "He has worked for us before."

"I do not think so."

"Why not?"

"Clint Adams is offering him something we cannot offer."

"And what is that?"

"The chance to stand with the Gunsmith in a fight."

"Perhaps," said Francisco, "we can offer him something Clint Adams cannot."

"Like what?"

"The chance to go against the Gunsmith."

Montoya gave that some thought, then said, "Perhaps."

Clint reined in Eclipse in front of Carmelita's and went inside. Rodrigo spotted him from behind the bar.

"Ah, *señor*," he said, "I am so very happy to see you."

"Alive, you mean?"

"*Sí, señor.*"

Clint looked around. Only one table was occupied at that moment.

"Can I get some food?"

"*Sí, señor*, of course," Rodrigo said. "I will tell my wife you are back."

"I'll just get cleaned up in my room," Clint said.

"Your food will be ready when you come back out. At the bar, or a table?"

"A table, since they're available," Clint said.

"As you wish, *señor.*"

Clint went to his room, poured some water in the basin, removed his shirt, and washed the trail dust from his body. He could have used a bath, but maybe he'd do that the next day.

By now Montoya probably knew about Piper, Autry, and Harker, but Clint knew very little about the man. There was no way he could predict what Montoya would do. Since Harker had already worked for Montoya in the past, he might try to buy the man off, but he'd have to find him first. And Clint was lucky that the three men were influenced by his reputation, were willing to stand with him and wait for their money.

After eating their evening meal, Inocencio Montoya pulled his brother aside and said, "I want to talk to Calderon."

"The sheriff? Why?"

"I want to know where he stands," Montoya said.

"I will have him brought here tomorrow morning."

"No," Montoya said, "tonight."

"Now?"

"Now."

Francisco sighed. When his brother made up his mind, there was no changing it.

"I will have someone ride into Acuña and get him."

Montoya slapped his brother on the back, and went to his desk.

After his meal Clint decided to spend the rest of the day in the cantina, drinking coffee and beer, waiting to see if Montoya was going to make a move before the day was over.

After dark, the three mercenaries came into the cantina.

Rodrigo, seeing three armed gringos enter the place, looked over at Clint, who nodded to him, immediately putting the Mexican's mind at ease.

Clint waved the three men over to his table. Rodrigo came over and Clint said, "Rodrigo, some food for my friends."

"*Sí, señor,*" Rodrigo said, "right away."

The three men sat, and Harker shook his head.

"I don't know how you can live that way," he said, speaking to Piper. He looked at Clint. "His house is falling apart, and he had nothing to eat there. I'm starvin'!"

"You'll like the food here," Clint assured him. "Best in town."

"He didn't even have anything to drink!"

"I gave you coffee," Piper argued.

"You called that coffee?"

"This is what I had to put up with all afternoon," Autry said. "You hear anything from Montoya?"

"Nothing," Clint said, "but I figure he knows about you three by now."

Piper looked at Harker.

"You worked for the man," he said. "What will he do?"

"He won't go off half-cocked," Harker said. "The man puts a lot of thought and planning into his moves."

"So we got nothing to worry about tonight," Autry said.

"I wouldn't say that," Harker said.

"What do you mean?" Clint asked.

"I ain't gonna spend the night in his house!" Harker said, pointing at Piper.

TWENTY

Calderon entered the Montoya house and came face-to-face with Francisco.

"This way, Sheriff."

Francisco led the lawman into the living room, where Inocencio was seated behind his desk.

"Sheriff Calderon," the rancher said. "Tequila?"

"Tequila would be good, *gracias, señor.*"

"Francisco, get our friend the sheriff a glass of tequila," Montoya said. "Sheriff, please have a seat."

Calderon sat down and accepted a glass from Francisco, who then stood off to the side.

"Thank you for coming, Sheriff."

"Did I have a choice?"

"Of course you did," Montoya said. "I just sent you an invitation."

An invitation from a Montoya was the same as a command, but Calderon didn't comment.

"Very well," Montoya said. "I will get to the point."

Calderon nodded and sipped his drink.

"You know three men named Piper, Autry, and Harker?"

"Gringo mercenaries," Calderon said. "They do most of their work in Mexico."

"How would Clint Adams know about them?"

"I did not know he did."

"Well, he does," Montoya said. "He has hired them to stand with him against my family."

"Do you know that for a fact?"

"I have good information that they are riding with him."

"Well," Calderon said, "they are all gringos."

"Are you saying that all gringos know each other?"

"Not all." Calderon finished his drink, leaned forward, and set the glass down on Montoya's desk.

"Sheriff," Montoya said, "I am going to kill Clint Adams."

"I have already heard that, *señor.*"

"And anyone who stands with him."

"That is too bad for them."

"What I need to know," Montoya said, "is where you will stand on all of this?"

"I will stand where I always stand, *señor,*" Calderon said, "on the side of the law. That is my job."

"A job you have because of me."

"I understand that, Señor Montoya," Calderon said, "but you gave me this job because you knew I would do it."

"Sheriff," Montoya said, "it would be unwise for you to stand between me and the man who shot my son."

"How is Juanito?"

"He is healing," Montoya said. "But his mother is making my life miserable."

"I am sorry to hear that."

"And she will continue to do that until I have killed the Gunsmith."

"*Señor,*" Calderon said, "I do not think the Gunsmith will die easily."

"I do not expect him to," Montoya said. "I just expect him to die."

* * *

Rodrigo covered the table with Carmelita's food, and the three mercenaries dug in. Clint decided to help them after he smelled it cooking.

"This town's got law, don't it?" Harker asked.

"It does," Clint said. "Sheriff Calderon."

"Is he in Montoya's pocket?"

"I don't think so," Clint said. "Not exactly anyway."

"What does that mean?" Piper asked.

"I don't think the sheriff will make a move until the dust settles."

"On us, you mean?" Autry asked.

"That's not the plan," Clint said. "I'm looking forward to paying all three of you."

"Shit," Piper said, "you really expect all of us to come out of this alive?"

Clint chewed the taco that was in his mouth, swallowed, and said, "That's the plan."

TWENTY-ONE

Francisco saw the sheriff to the front door, then returned to the living room. His brother was still seated behind his desk, deep in thought.

"What do you think, my brother?" Francisco asked.

"I do not think we will have any trouble with him," Montoya said without looking at his brother.

"Why not?"

Now Inocencio looked at his brother.

"He knows better than to stand in my way."

"And what if he decides to try and act like a real lawman?" Francisco asked.

Montoya looked at his brother again.

"Then we would take the badge away from him."

Francisco nodded.

"Why don't you turn in, Francisco?" Montoya suggested.

"And you?"

"I will be here for a while," Montoya said.

"Very well," Francisco said. "*Buenas tardes*."

"*Buenas tardes*," Montoya said.

Clint got Harker his own room in the back of Carmelita's. Rodrigo said he had a cousin who had a room in the back of his store, so he rented it for Piper and Autry. That way, they could be close by.

After Carmelita's closed, Rodrigo remained behind the bar to give Clint and Harker beers. Carmelita finished cleaning the kitchen and went to bed.

After a couple of hours, Rodrigo came over to their table.

"*Señors*, I will go to bed now, so I can open early in the morning," he said. "Help yourselves to *cerveza*."

"*Gracias*, Rodrigo," Clint said. "We'll make sure we don't drink you out of business."

"*Gracias, señor. Buenas tardes.*"

Rodrigo went down the hall to the rooms he shared with Carmelita.

"That feller is real impressed with you," Harker said.

"He's a good friend."

"But he ain't the kind of friend you really need right now," Harker said.

"The kinds of friends I need are the kinds who cost me a thousand dollars each."

"Ain't you got cheaper friends?"

"Probably," Clint said, "if I could get to a telegraph office. But then it would take time to get to them, and time for them to get here. This way's easier."

"You really make that money playing poker?"

"I did," Clint said. "I got lucky."

"I'd like that kind of luck," Harker said, "making thousands of dollars without gettin' shot at."

"Sometimes you lose, though."

"Well then," Harker said, "it's about the same as gettin' shot at, ain't it?"

"Pretty much."

"Can I ask you a question?"

"Go ahead."

"Why didn't you just kill the Montoya kid, and ride out?"

"There was no reason to kill him," Clint said. "He wasn't half as good with a gun as he thought he was."

"That the only reason?"

"What other reason could there be?" Clint asked. "I don't kill unless I have to."

"That ain't exactly what your reputation says about you," Harker pointed out.

"I can't help that," Clint said. "I have to live up to my own standards, not the standards others have tried to set for me."

Harker finished his beer and stared into the mug.

"You want another?" he asked Clint.

"One more, and then I'm goin' to bed."

"We gonna set a watch?" Harker asked as he walked to the bar.

"I don't think so," Clint said. "Not yet anyway. Montoya is still thinking."

Harker went behind the bar, drew two more beers, and carried them back to the table. He set one down in front of Clint, then sat back down.

"You really feel that way?" he asked.

"What way?"

"That you don't have to live up to your reputation?"

"I have to be aware of it," Clint said. "I don't have to live by it."

"I've met lots of men with reputations," Harker said. "Most of them let it go to their heads."

"Let me guess," Clint said. "Most of those men are dead."

"Yup."

"What about you?" Clint asked. "You've got a reputation, don't you?"

"Just for doin' what I say I'm gonna do," Harker replied, "or what I'm paid to do."

"Since you worked for Montoya before," Clint said, "what would happen if he tried to buy you? Made you a better offer than I did?"

"Can't happen."

"Why not?"

"Well, first, I already made a deal with you," Harker said. "I don't go back on deals."

"You said *first*," Clint said. "What's second?"

"I don't like Montoya."

"Why not?"

"I worked for him once."

"And?"

"He tried not to pay me."

"How did that go?"

"He claimed I didn't do the job he hired me for," Harker said. "And I mean, the whole job."

"And?"

"And he was wrong."

"And he paid you?"

Harker nodded.

"I made him see the error of his ways, and convinced him that it would be a bad idea not to pay me."

"So my guess is," Clint said, "if you don't like him, he doesn't like you."

"Good guess."

"So maybe he wants to kill you as much as he wants to kill me?" Clint suggested.

"I doubt it," Harker said. "All I did was make him pay me what he owed me. I didn't shoot his son. No, I think you're still number one on his list."

"Thanks for that." Clint drank down half the beer, then pushed the rest away. "I'm going to bed."

"I'll finish my beer, then put both mugs back behind the bar," Harker said.

Clint said, "Good night." He stood up, walked to the doorway that led to the hall, then turned back. "You're going to stay on watch, aren't you?"

"I thought I might," Harker said, "for a while."

"Okay," Clint said, "I'll relieve you in four hours."

TWENTY-TWO

Francisco Montoya was in his room when there was a knock on his door. He opened it, and Maria Montoya, his sister-in-law, slipped inside. She was wearing a robe.

"Where is Inocencio?" she asked.

"At his desk," Francisco said. "He has work to do."

"Then he will be there for a while?"

"Yes," Francisco said, "likely most of the night. How is Juanito?"

"Asleep."

"Then we are safe."

She shrugged and the robe fell to the floor, revealing her to be naked. She was once a slender beauty, but with large breasts. Now in her fifties she had become a voluptuous beauty, with large breasts and wide hips, full buttocks and thighs. Francisco still found her to be the most beautiful thing he had ever seen, just as he had the first day his brother had brought her home thirty years before. They had only begun to sleep together two years earlier. Neither had planned it, but now they had no way of stopping it.

He took her into his arms and kissed her, his hands roaming over her body, down her back until he was clutching her ass cheeks, pulling her to him. He kissed her hungrily, while

her hands snaked between them to undo his trousers. When
they dropped to the floor, he stepped out of them, then lifted
her and carried her to the bed. By the time he dropped her
on it, his cock was fully erect.

He climbed on the bed with her, positioned himself
between her legs, and drove himself into her. Being with
each other in the house of Inocencio Montoya meant they
didn't have much time for anything else.

Downstairs Inocencio Montoya poured himself another
glass of tequila and sat back in his chair. It was no surprise
that Clint Adams had gone out and gotten himself some
help. However, it did surprise him that the Gunsmith had
hired mercenaries. He knew Mel Harker was a hard man.
From everything he knew about the other two, Piper and
Autry, they were also hard.

Montoya knew he and his family could kill them. They
would overwhelm them with numbers, but in the doing of
it, they might lose more than a few cousins. So perhaps he
needed more than just family members for this.

Perhaps he needed some mercenaries of his own.

He looked up at the ceiling. He knew what was probably
going on upstairs. His brother and his wife thought he didn't
know what was going on, but he did. He just wasn't ready
to make them pay—yet. But they would, both of them, when
the time was right.

He took out a piece of paper, dipped a quill into an ink-
well, and began to write. Mexico had its own mercenaries,
its own hard men who would match up very well with the
hard gringos.

When Sheriff Calderon reached the small house that had
come with the badge, he went inside and lit a lamp. He
removed his gun, took the badge from his shirt, and dropped
it on the table next to the lamp. It was dull, having long since
lost its shine. The badge had been handed down from sheriff

to sheriff over many years. Many men had died wearing that badge, and he had no desire to be one of them.

He washed himself and got ready for bed. First, though, he poured himself a glass of tequila and drank it slowly.

He had no intentions of getting between Inocencio Montoya and Clint Adams. All that would do was get him riddled with bullets. Another dead man with a badge.

What he would do when it was all over, however, depended on who came out of it alive.

He was hungry. He had no wife to cook for him, so he had to eat some old tacos he had in his kitchen. After washing them down with more tequila, he then went to his small bedroom. In bed, under the covers, he laced his hands behind his head and stared at the ceiling. Perhaps his time in this job was ready to end. Maybe another man would hire some deputies and try to stop the coming gun battle, but that idea just did not appeal to him.

His badge was lying on the table in the living room next to the lamp. Maybe the thing to do come morning was just walk out of the house and ride away, leaving that badge right where it was.

TWENTY-THREE

Clint took the last watch.

Even though he didn't think it was necessary, he couldn't very well make Harker sit up all night, so he relieved him after four hours and let the man go to sleep.

He was still sitting at the table when Carmelita came into the cantina.

"*Señor*," she said, "have you been there all night?"

"No," he said, "only half."

"You must need coffee."

"Yes, thank you," he said. "A lot of it."

"I will bring it right out."

Before long the good strong smell of coffee filled the place, and then she carried a pot and a mug to him and set them down on the table.

"*Gracias*, Carmelita," he said.

"I can make you some breakfast."

"I'll wait for my friends to arrive," he said. "Just do what you normally do in the morning."

"I must ready the kitchen for the day."

"Then don't let me stop you," he said.

She smiled at him and went back into the kitchen.

*   *   *

Rodrigo came out about an hour later, bade Clint good morning, and went into the kitchen to help his wife.

Mel Harker came out next, sat down with Clint, and poured some coffee into a mug Rodrigo had brought out for him.

"Breakfast?" Rodrigo asked.

Harker looked at Clint.

"We'll wait for our other friends," Clint said. "They should be here soon."

"Sí, señor."

When Rodrigo opened the front doors for the business day to start, the first ones through the door were Willie Piper and Jed Autry.

Rodrigo brought out more coffee, and all four men asked him to bring breakfast.

"Just bring everything," Autry said. The big man had a huge appetite.

"You fellas sleep all right?" Harker asked. He was looking at Autry. "Your eyes are red."

"He snores," Autry said sourly.

"Why am I not surprised?" Harker asked.

"Hey, I can't help it," Piper said. "Besides, I'm used to living alone."

"I think I know why," Autry said.

"What's that mean?" Piper demanded.

"It means I don't think you could get a woman to live with you," Harker said.

"I wouldn't want no woman to live with me," Piper said. "Females is more trouble than they're worth."

"No they ain't," Autry said.

"I've got to agree," Clint said.

"Women," Piper grumbled as if it were a dirty word.

"A woman cooked all this food," Harker said.

"And that's probably all they're good for," Piper said.

"Don't let a woman who cooks your food hear you say that," Harker advised.

Piper looked down at the breakfast burrito in his hand, then said, "Awww," and bit into it.

After breakfast, Autry asked Clint what his plan was.

"Well, I was thinking about waiting for Montoya to make his move," Clint said, "but now I'm thinking, why wait? Why give him the first move?" He looked at Harker. "You said he never moves until he's looked at all the angles."

"I said something like that, yeah."

"Well," Clint said, "maybe we should take that time away from him."

"How do you plan to do that?" Piper asked.

"By going to see him."

"You're gonna ride right into the lion's den?" Autry asked.

"We all are," Clint said.

"All of us?" Piper asked. "Riding right up to his house?"

Clint looked at Harker.

"He won't be ready for us, right? Won't have all his family gathered?"

"Probably not," Harker said, "but . . ."

"But what?" Clint asked.

"Well, you're the boss of this outfit, but . . ."

"Go ahead," Clint said. "I'll listen to anybody's comments."

"We gotta figure that Montoya knows about the three of us by now," Harker said. "That we're ridin' with you."

"That's the way I figure it."

"Well, he's got to know that his family might not fare so well against four pros," Harker said. "All he'll have on his side are numbers."

"I'd put the four of us up against a bunch of amateurs any day," Autry said.

"That's my point," Harker said.

"What?"

"I get it," Clint said. "You think since I hired some pros, he's going to do the same."

"That's what I figure."

"Who would he hire?"

"Mexicans."

"Mexican mercenaries?" Clint asked. "Are there a lot around here?"

"We're in Mexico, Clint," Harker said. "There's plenty."

TWENTY-FOUR

Inocencio Montoya looked up from the table as Francisco entered the dining room.

"Good morning," he said.

"Good morning," Francisco said. He looked around. "Is Maria coming down for breakfast?"

"She is with Juanito," Montoya said. "They are having breakfast together in his room, so it is just you and I, my brother."

"Ah . . . *bueno*," Francisco said, sitting down.

The cook, a middle-aged Mexican woman named Conchita, brought out platters of food—eggs, refried beans, ham, tortillas—and the two men began to eat.

"What are your plans today?" Francisco asked. "Did you think of a plan last night?"

"Roberto Del Plata."

Francisco was in the act of reaching for a tortilla, but stopped when he heard the name.

"Roberto? But . . . you hate each other."

"Right now, not as much as I hate Clint Adams," Montoya said.

"But he hates you."

"For enough money he will put that aside," Montoya said.

"Possibly," Francisco said.

Montoya grabbed some eggs and ham—the cook made them especially for him, since he liked them so much—and rolled them up in a tortilla. He took a bite and chewed.

"What will you have him do?" his brother asked.

"Hire five other men," Montoya said. "We need professional guns to combat professional guns."

"The Gunsmith will not expect that?"

"He might," Montoya said. "Harker certainly will."

"That man," Francisco said. "You should have killed him last time, instead of paying him."

"You might be right," Montoya said. "Lately I find I am not killing the people I should be killing when they deserve to be killed."

Once again Francisco stopped himself before biting into his food. What did his brother mean by that?

"After breakfast I want you and Mejías to find him." Mejías was the foreman of Montoya's ranch, his *segundo.* "Bring him here. I will allow him to choose the men we hire."

"As you wish."

"What is your problem with this?" Montoya asked.

"We usually handle family business ourselves."

"I know that," Montoya said. "I am the one who makes sure of that, but in this case we cannot depend on our family to handle these mercenaries. We need professionals."

"Yes, of course," Francisco said.

"This will save the lives of some of our sons and cousins, Francisco," Montoya went on, "but will see to it that our family business gets done."

"Of course you are right, Inocencio," Francisco said. His brother's previous statement still bothered him. Did he know? Did Inocencio know about his brother and his wife? No, he certainly would have said something long before this.

After breakfast, Montoya rose and said, "I am going to look in on Juanito. You and Mejías get Del Plata here quickly."

"I will do that immediately," Francisco said.

He left the dining room with his brother, then stood there and watched as Montoya went up the stairs and disappeared down the hall. Reluctantly, Francisco opened the door and went out.

Francisco found Mejías by the corral, watching one of the men work a pony. He told the man what Montoya's orders were.

"Roberto Del Plata?" Enrique Mejías asked. "But . . . he hates the boss."

"And the boss hates him," Francisco added, "but my brother feels we need him."

Mejías shrugged and said, "Well, better Del Plata than some of our own hands. Our men are *vaqueros*, not gunmen."

"And we have no gunmen in the family either," Francisco said. "So Inocencio feels we need some professional guns."

"Del Plata is possibly the fastest gun in all of Mexico," Mejías said. "I would like to see him face the Gunsmith."

"So would I," Francisco said, "and that is probably what will happen."

Mejías called one of the other men over, gave him some instructions, then said to Francisco, "I will saddle the horses."

"I will meet you at the barn," Francisco said. "I am going to get my rifle from my room."

"Bueno."

As Inocencio Montoya entered his son's room, Maria Montoya turned her head to look at him, then looked away. These days she could barely stand the sight of her husband.

For his part, Montoya wondered if he should just kill her now, in front of her son. It might teach him a lesson about loyalty. If he'd had his gun on him at that moment, he might have shot her.

He knew his brother and wife were rutting behind his back. What he had a hard time deciding was whether to kill one or both of them. And if it was one, which one? Which

was the bigger betrayal? And going forward with his ranch
and his business, which of them did he need the most?

Maria was holding her son's hand, and Montoya knew
that if he did not do something soon, the boy would be a
hopeless momma's boy.

So in the end, that might have been the deciding factor
in Montoya's decision to kill his wife. Now the only question was . . . when?

TWENTY-FIVE

Clint finally got the three mercenaries to agree to his plan. He did not want to force any of them to ride with him if they weren't on board.

They all saddled their horses and met in front of Carmelita's Cantina.

Piper leaned over to Harker while they were waiting for Clint to come out and asked, "What if we're ridin' into a hornet's nest?"

"Should be fun," Harker said.

"You're a crazy man," Piper said. "I don't do this for fun. This is business."

"If you really felt that way," Autry said, "you wouldn't even be in that saddle unless you got paid up front."

"Well," Piper said grudgingly, "the chance to ride with the Gunsmith . . ."

"We get it," Harker said.

Clint Adams came out of the cantina and the three mercenaries fell silent.

"Ready?" Clint asked.

"As ready as we'll ever be," Harker said.

"Now remember," Clint said, mounting up, "no gunplay unless they initiate it."

"Seems to me we'd intimidate them more with some gunplay," Autry said. "I mean, we are looking to intimidate them, right?"

"Why don't we just shoot up the place?" Piper asked.

Clint turned Eclipse so he could face all three men.

"This is not fun for me," he said. "If we can get through this without firing a shot, I'd prefer it."

"And if we don't fire a shot," Harker said, "if we ride in there and they back down today, we still get paid, right?"

"That's right," Clint said. "This is not blood money. You get paid simply for backing my play—whatever that play is."

"Well, let's go, then," Piper said. "Sooner we get this over with, the better for everybody."

"Amen," Clint said. He pointed at Harker. "You've been out there before, so you lead the way."

"Got it."

They left Acuña single file . . .

Inocencio Montoya looked up as his younger son, Pablo, came barreling into the room, looking wild-eyed.

"What is it?" Montoya asked. "What is wrong?"

"He is coming, Papa."

"Who is coming?"

"Clint Adams," Pablo said. "The Gunsmith. He is coming."

"Here? Now?"

"He is almost here!"

"Is he alone?"

"No, Papa. He has three riders with him."

"All right." Montoya stood.

"Should I get the men—"

"No," Montoya said. "No men, and no guns. Leave yours here."

"B-But Papa—"

"Leave your gun here, Pablito," Montoya said. He only called Pablo "Pablito" when he was deadly serious.

"Yes, Papa." Pablo removed his weapon and the bandolero he wore.

"Now we go out," Montoya said.

As Clint and his mercenaries approached the house, some of the *vaqueros* stopped their work to look at them.

"They're not armed," Clint pointed out.

"They never are," Harker pointed out. "They are *vaqueros*, not gunmen."

As they got closer, the front door opened and Montoya stepped out with his younger son by his side. Neither man was wearing a gun.

"See anything?" Clint asked.

"Nothing," Piper said.

"Me neither," Autry said. "Doesn't look like we're covered from any direction."

"Okay," Clint said.

When they reached the house, they reined in their horses, stood four abreast.

"Señor Montoya," Clint said.

"Señor Adams," Montoya said. "To what do we owe this visit? Have you and your mercenaries come to shoot up my ranchero?"

"Nobody's shooting anything up, *señor*," Clint said. "I just wanted you to know that whatever you are planning, I will not be alone."

"Judging from the company you are keeping," Montoya said, "you have hired some professional help."

"These men have been hired, yes," Clint said, "to back me in the event you and your family come for me."

Montoya grinned.

"I would have thought the infamous gringo Gunsmith would have no trouble facing twenty Mexicans."

"I am not so foolish as to believe my own reputation, Señor Montoya," Clint said. "No man can stand alone against twenty."

"You are a wise man, then," Montoya said.

"Perhaps," Clint said. "Maybe a wise man would have left town by now."

"Leaving town would not help you," Montoya said. "I would track you."

"That's what I figured," Clint said. "Better to resolve this issue than try to walk away from it."

Montoya's son, standing next to him, was fidgeting nervously. Clint was glad the young man wasn't wearing a gun. He might have done something foolish.

Montoya looked at Harker.

"Señor Harker," he said, "it has been a while."

"Yes, it has."

"Do you think this is a wise move for you?"

"I'm gettin' paid to do a job," Harker said. "I never claimed to be a wise man."

"I recognize these other two men," Montoya said. "Señors Piper and Autry, no?"

Neither man responded, so Clint said, "That's right."

Montoya nodded and said, "I see. Well, you came here to inform me, and I am informed. Now, unless you plan to kill me now as I am unarmed, I have work to do."

"Change your mind, Montoya," Clint said. "That's my advice to you. No one in your family has died . . . yet."

"I will take your advice under consideration, *señor*," Montoya said. "But I will give you some advice, as well."

"I'm listening."

"Make peace with your God," Montoya said, "whoever that may be. All of you."

Harker turned his horse so that Montoya could see the gun on his hip.

"This is my only God," he said, placing his hand on his gun, "and I am very much at peace with it."

"Very well, then," Montoya said. "I will see you all . . . very soon."

TWENTY-SIX

Riding back to Acuña, Harker asked, "Did that accomplish what you wanted?"

"Well," Clint said, "he saw the four of us together, so yes, it did."

"He didn't look particularly impressed," Autry said.

"Or scared," Piper said.

"Well," Clint said, "according to Harker, who has worked for him before, even if Montoya was scared, it wouldn't show."

"That's right," Harker said. "He could be pissin' in his pants, but you wouldn't see the wet."

"So let's just assume he's going to react," Clint said, "probably by hiring some guns of his own."

"So then what do we do?" Autry asked. "Hire us some more? And then he hires some more? Where does that stop?"

"Here," Clint said, "it stops here. We're it. I'm not hiring any more guns."

"Okay, then," Harker said. "So where do we go from here?"

"I have some ideas," Clint said, "but let me think about it for a while."

"What's 'a while'?" Autry asked.

"Overnight," Clint said. "By tomorrow I should have an idea about what I want to do."

"Or what we should do?" Harker asked.

"Right," Clint said, "what we should do."

"Just so long as you don't tell us we got to die," Piper said, "because if that happens, I wanna go down fightin'."

"Believe me," Clint said. "My plan is for all of us to come out of this alive."

Francisco and Mejías found Roberto Del Plata in a cantina in a collection of buildings that was less a town than a mud-hole in the road.

"Ah," Del Plata said as they entered, "Francisco Montoya. And the Montoya *segundo*." He was sitting at a table with two women who were wearing peasant blouses, displaying wares that had seen better days.

"Do you want a drink?" Del Plata asked.

"A drink would be fine," Francisco said. "*Cerveza, por favor*."

"Mejías?" Del Plata said.

"Same."

"Enrique," Del Plata snapped. "*Dos cervezas por mis amigos*." He looked at them and said in English, "Sit."

Francisco and Mejías sat and the bartender brought over their beers.

"Now to what do I owe this honor?" Del Plata asked.

Roberto Del Plata was a handsome man in his late thirties. He'd been a bandito for many years, then turned his considerable talents to mercenary work. When he had enough money for tequila and women, he took time off. When the money was gone, he went back to work. He was satisfied with that life.

"We are here at the behest of Don Inocencio," Francisco said. "My brother."

"Your brother," Del Plata said with a smirk. "Why do I have the feeling you hate your brother almost as much as I do?"

"That is not true."

"Perhaps not," Del Plata said. "Perhaps a little less, eh?"

Francisco didn't respond, but just sipped his beer.

"Very well, then," Del Plata said, "what does Don Inocencio want from me?"

"He wants to give you a job."

"A job?" Del Plata said. "As a *vaquero* maybe?"

"No," Francisco said, "he wants to hire you to do what you do best."

"What is it Don Inocencio thinks I do best?"

Francisco raised his mug in a toast and said, "Kill."

Del Plata sipped some tequila and seemed to consider that answer.

"*Bueno*," he said finally. "At least the man remembers what I am good at."

"He remembers," Francisco said.

"Then tell me, Francisco," Del Plata said, "who does your brother want me to kill?"

Francisco hesitated, then said, "The Gunsmith."

TWENTY-SEVEN

When Clint and his mercenaries reached Acuña, they went directly to Carmelita's. Rodrigo and his wife were cleaning up after the afternoon meal.

"*Señor*," Rodrigo said. "Good to see you."

"Why do I have the feeling, Rodrigo, my friend," Clint asked, "that every time I go out that door, you think I'm going to get killed?"

"I am just happy to see you safe. Sit, I will bring food."

"Sounds good to me," Autry said.

They sat. Rodrigo got them beers, and then went into the kitchen to tell his wife to start cooking again.

"You found yourself a real good headquarters here, Clint," Harker said.

"Yeah," Piper said, "it ain't half bad."

When Rodrigo reappeared, he was carrying trays of food. He had with him a woman, also carrying food. They set the trays on the table, passed out plates to each man.

"This is my wife's little sister, Raquel."

Clint looked at Raquel. All she had in common with her sister was a pretty face and smooth skin. Raquel was probably a hundred pounds lighter, her shapely body on display in a simple skirt and peasant blouse.

"*Hola*," she said with a smile.

"Hello," Clint said.

She and Rodrigo went back to the kitchen.

"She likes you," Autry said.

"You can tell that from hello?" Piper asked.

"I know women," Autry said. He looked at Clint. "You're gonna be busy tonight."

"We'll see," Clint said. "Right now I want to be busy eating."

"I'm with you there," Harker said, and they dug in.

They didn't have to go far to find Del Plata's men. They were in the same mudhole.

Francisco and Mejías waited in the cantina while Del Plata went to the whorehouse to get his men.

"I hope these men are good enough," Francisco said to Mejías.

"If they are working for Del Plata, then they are good enough," the foreman said.

"They better be," Francisco said. "Don Inocencio will not be happy if they fail us."

"Don Inocencio is never happy these days."

"*Silencio!*"

Mejías looked at Francisco. They had known each other a long time.

"I am not telling you anything you do not already know," Mejías said. "The *patrón* is an unhappy man."

"Well, he is not any happier these days," Francisco said, "not with Juanito being shot."

"He will be happier when he has killed the Gunsmith," Mejías said. "But I thought he wanted the family to do it."

"That was when the Gunsmith was standing alone," Francisco said. "Now he has three gringo mercenaries with him."

"I thought I saw Harker with him," Mejías said. "Who are the others?"

"Piper and Autry."

"Good men."

"So it will take good men to defeat them," Francisco said.

"And not family."

Francisco nodded.

Del Plata came in at that point, followed by four men. They were all dressed like banditos, and armed to the teeth. Almost everything a bandito wore was a weapon, or could be used as one.

"These are your men?" Francisco asked.

"*Sí.*"

The men all smiled at Francisco, several of them revealing gaps where teeth used to be, others showing gold teeth.

"Very well," he said, standing. "We must ride to the ranchero."

"I believe my men would like some money first," Del Plata said.

"First we ride to the ranchero," Francisco said. "I'm sure Don Inocencio will be willing to pay some money to your men."

Del Plata looked at his men, then at Francisco.

"All right," he said. "We ride."

TWENTY-EIGHT

Clint was starting to think that Autry was right.

Each time Carmelita's sister, Raquel, came to the table with more food or beer, she made sure that her hip made solid contact with Clint's shoulder.

By the end of the meal, his shoulder was warm from her hip.

"See?" Autry leaned over and said. "I told you. I know women. That one's going to be warming your bed tonight."

"All we've said to each other is hello."

"That doesn't matter," Autry said, "and I think you know that as well as I do."

Clint did. He had ended up in bed in the past with women he had exchanged no words with. Sometimes all it took was a look. Or the touch of a hip.

But going to bed was a long way off. There was plenty of the day left ahead.

He spoke to the whole table.

"What kind of contacts have you fellas got in Mexico?" he asked the three mercenaries.

"Mine aren't as good as these two have," Harker said, "but I've got some."

"I got some," Piper said.

"I've got a few more," Autry said.

"Why?" Harker asked Clint.

"I thought maybe we'd get ahead of the game by finding out who Montoya is hiring."

"What makes you think the word will get out?" Piper asked.

"He's going to have to offer a lot of money for the right men," Clint said. "That kind of thing has a habit of getting around."

"He's got a point," Autry said. "Okay, I'll ask around."

"Me, too."

"I'll stay with Clint," Harker said.

"Why?" Clint asked.

"Somebody's got to watch your back."

"I'd rather you get in touch with your contacts," Clint said. "I'll be okay here until you get back."

"What are you gonna do here?" Piper asked.

"Like I said before," Clint answered, "I've got an idea, but I want to refine it before I tell it to you."

"Tomorrow, then?"

"Yes," Clint said, "tomorrow."

"Okay," Piper said. "I guess we'll be seeing you later."

Piper and Autry walked out. Harker stood, but didn't leave right away.

"You sure about this?"

"Why wouldn't I be sure?"

"We don't want to come back here and find you dead," Harker said. "That way, nobody gets paid."

"I'll be fine."

Harker left. As he did, Carmelita came out of the kitchen with a fresh pot of coffee and poured some into Clint's empty cup.

"You know," she said to him, "my sister is not married."

Del Plato's men remained outside with Mejías while Francisco took him inside to talk to Don Inocencio.

"That will be all, Francisco," Montoya said to his brother.

"But Inocencio—"

"You can wait outside with Señor Del Plato's men."

Del Plato sat down, crossed his legs, and hung his hat on the toe of his boot.

"Don Inocencio," he said, "how nice it was to hear from you again."

"Tequila?"

"Of course."

Montoya poured a glass and handed it to Del Plato. He did not have one himself. He was particular about whom he drank with. Instead, he went to his desk and sat down.

"Francisco told me about the Gunsmith," Del Plato said. "Shall we go into town and take care of him now?"

"Not yet," Montoya said, "but when we do go, we will be going with you."

"We?"

"The family."

"Ah."

"Did you bring good men?"

"The best." Del Plato sipped his drink. "They are outside. Would you like to see them?"

"Later," Montoya said. "I trust your judgment."

"*Bueno.* How is Juanito?"

"Healing."

"How did he get shot?"

"By being a damned fool."

"That boy needs a tight rein."

"Do not tell me how to—" Montoya bit his tongue. This was not the time. "Yes, he does. But we're not here to talk about my son."

"But we are, aren't we?" Del Plata asked. "Or at least, the man who shot him."

"Yes," Montoya said, "Clint Adams."

"The Gunsmith," Del Plata said, "here in Acuña. What is he doing here?"

"I do not know why he came," Montoya said, "only that he shot Juanito while he was here. For that he must pay."

"Die, you mean."

"Exactly."

"Francisco said you want you and your family to be there when he dies."

"Not be there," Montoya said. "Take part in killing him."

"Why don't you and your brother and sons just go and kill him? Surely you outnumber him."

"We did," Montoya said, "but not anymore. He has help."

Del Plata laughed.

"Who did he get in Acuña stupid enough to go up against you?" he asked.

"Countrymen of his," Montoya said. "Mercenaries. Men named Piper, Autry, and Harker."

"I know Harker," Del Plata said. "He worked for you once."

"Yes, he did."

"And I know of the other two," Del Plata said. "They are fighting men."

"And so are your men," Montoya said.

"So you think you have evened the odds by hiring me and my men?" Del Plata said.

"That is what I think."

"Well, you may be right, at that," Del Plata said, "but before my men will move against a man like the Gunsmith, they'll want to see some money."

Montoya opened his top drawer, took out a bulging brown envelope, and tossed it to Del Plata's side of the desk.

"Will that be sufficient?"

Del Plata picked up the envelope and riffled through the currency inside.

"*Sí, señor,*" he said, "this will do it nicely."

"Pass it out any way you see fit," Montoya said.

"*Señor,*" Del Plata asked, "when will we be going after the Gunsmith?"

"Tomorrow, I think," Montoya said. "I think we shall kill the Gunsmith tomorrow."

TWENTY-NINE

Clint ate once again at Carmelita's later that evening. He swore he must have gained twenty pounds just during the few days he was in Acuña.

The three mercenaries did not return, but that was okay. He expected to see them in the morning.

He retired to his room early, because he still had a lot of thinking to do. As he had told the three men, he had an idea, but he wasn't sure about it. He needed to sleep on it.

He had his boots and shirt off and was reading by the light of his lamp, as it had long been dark out, when there was a knock at his door. It could have been any of the mercenaries, it could have been Rodrigo, but he still went to the door with his gun in his hand.

When he opened the door, he saw Raquel standing in the hall, with her hands behind her back.

"Raquel?"

"*Señor,*" she said, "can I do something for you?"

"Um, I don't really need anything—"

"I can do something you want, perhaps?"

He was about to tell her no when he remembered what Autry had said. She had a smile on her pretty face, and her hair gleamed as if she had just washed it. When the smell of her reached him, he knew she was fresh from a bath.

"Raquel—"

"Can I come in?" she asked, looking up and down the hall. She was concerned about being seen.

"Of course."

He stepped back to let her in, then closed the door. She turned to face him, giving him a sloe-eyed look. It was obvious what she had on her mind, and who was he to disappoint her?

But there was one thing.

"Does your sister know you're here?" he asked. "And more important, does your brother-in-law know? I don't want him coming in here with a rifle."

She did a little wriggle thing with her shoulders, and the peasant blouse—already off the shoulder and halfway down her arms—fell to her waist. Her large bare breasts were beautiful, with perfectly shaped rounded undersides, and dark brown nipples.

"Do you really care?"

He was aware that his mouth was hanging open, so he closed it.

She pulled the blouse up over her head and tossed it away, then dropped her skirt to the floor and kicked it, making her breasts bobble a bit. The tangle of black hair between her legs was dense, but he knew what was beneath it.

"You don't need that gun, Señor Clint," she said.

"As long as we know Rodrigo isn't coming in here, guns blazing."

"Do not worry," she said. "I promise you no one will interrupt us." She put her arms out. "Now come to me."

He put his gun back in the holster hanging on the bedpost, then did as she asked. She wrapped her arms around him, pressed her bare breasts to his bare chest, and kissed him hungrily.

Her hands moved over him, undoing his trousers with

great dexterity. She was obviously an experienced girl, and while she was Carmelita's little sister, she was perhaps not as young as she appeared to be.

He stepped back and reached for her breasts, held them in his hands, and lifted them to his mouth. He feasted on her dark nipples, taking them in his mouth, nibbling them, sucking them, making her moan and clutch at his head.

They staggered back toward the bed together, but before they could fall onto it, she leaped up and wrapped her legs around his waist, her arms grabbing on to him around the neck. He held her tightly, his hard, erect penis caught between them. She rubbed her pubic bush up and down on him, then leaned back and brought him down on the bed on top of her.

He was reveling in the smell of her. Although she was fresh from a bath, there was also an earthy odor to her skin, and another, special odor from between her legs.

As he kissed her body, she put her hands up over her head and stretched luxuriously. He pressed his face between her breasts and breathed her in, then kissed his way down to her belly, licked her navel, then kept moving down. Her thighs were smooth, and he couldn't help thinking she was Carmelita, but years ago. She had the same brown, smooth skin, the same lustrous hair.

He kissed her thighs, saving the best taste for last . . .

The three mercenaries met in a small cantina at the other end of Acuña. They wanted to talk to each other without Clint Adams around.

They had a beer each and exchanged information they'd gotten from their contacts.

It all came down to the same thing.

Roberto Del Plata . . .

"I know Del Plata has worked for Montoya before," Harker said. "He has a good crew."

"So they won't recruit anyone else?" Piper asked.

"I don't think so," Harker said. "He's got his own men, and they're all good."

"So now we're facing more than just Montoya and his family," Autry said.

"I don't like it," Piper said. "We need to talk to Clint."

"About what?" Autry asked. "Runnin'?"

"No," Harker said, "he wouldn't run any more than we would. I think I know what Piper means."

"Go ahead," Piper said.

"We need to pick the ground," Harker said.

"Choose our own battlefield," Piper said.

"And that means . . ." Harker said.

"Leaving Mexico," Autry said.

They both looked at Piper.

"Hey," he said with a shrug, "that works for me."

THIRTY

Clint's face was not so much buried in Raquel's crotch as it was *burrowed* in. The combination of the fresh-from-the-bath smell and her own earthy, sweet-sour odor was heady.

She was gasping and actually growling as he worked on her with his lips and tongue. She lifted her knees to spread herself even more for him, and kept her hands on the back of his head. When she knew she was going to scream, she turned her head and tried to bury it in the pillow, only partially succeeding . . .

"Montoya will not be comfortable in Texas," Harker said. "This I know."

"Well, we want him uncomfortable, that's for sure," Piper said.

"What about Del Plata?" Autry asked. "Will he be uncomfortable, as well?"

"No," Harker said, "he's a fighting man, he'll fight anywhere. But Montoya's in charge. This will throw him off."

"So," Piper said, "we only need to convince Clint to take the fight to Texas, and that it will not be the same as runnin'."

"I don't think that will be hard," Harker said. "He's a smart man."

"I hope you're right," Piper said, "because in the end he's gonna call the shots. If he says stay, we'll have to stay."

"We could walk away," Autry offered.

"And which of us is going to do that?"

"Not me," Autry said. "I wouldn't want to miss the fun."

"Me neither," Harker said.

"You guys are nuts," Piper said. "This ain't gonna be fun. Killin' ain't fun."

"Maybe not," Autry said, "but fightin' is."

He and Harker clinked mugs and drank.

"What'ya suppose Clint's doin' now?" Piper said. "Maybe we better go over there."

"I don't think so," Autry said. "That little Mex gal's got his pants off by now."

"You back talkin' about that again?" Piper asked. "How do you know that?"

"I told you," Autry said. "I know women."

Piper shook his head and said, "I'm gonna get some tequila. Anybody?"

"Another beer," Autry said.

"Me, too," Harker said.

"Comin' up."

Piper got up and went to the bar.

"How much do you know about him?" Harker asked.

"A lot," Autry said. "He's a good man."

"That's good to know."

"I don't know that much about you, though," Autry said.

"Well," Harker said, "I'm a fighting man, just like you two."

Piper returned with the drinks.

"Whatayall talkin' about?"

"You," Autry said.

"Fightin' men," Harker said.

"Speakin' of which," Piper said, "what about Del Plata? I've heard about him, but never seen him."

"He's a good man," Harker said, "good with a gun, a knife, and his hands."

"Good with a gun?" Autry asked. "We talkin' Gunsmith good?"

"None of us are Gunsmith good," Harker said, "but I don't think it's gonna be that kind of fight."

"No," Piper said, "this should be a helluva bloodbath, nothing *mano a mano*."

"I don't think anybody wants to go *mano a mano* with Clint Adams," Harker said.

"I sure don't," Autry said.

"You think he's as fast as his reputation says he is?" Harker asked.

"Who knows?" Autry said. "He sure don't flaunt it, though."

"No, he don't," Piper said, "but I think he only has to be half as fast as they say he is."

"For our sakes," Harker said, "I hope he is."

"Let's drink to that," Autry said.

THIRTY-ONE

When Clint woke up, Raquel was lying on her side with her back to him. He looked at the window, and although it would never get any direct sunlight, there was no light at all. It was nowhere near time to get up.

He had a full erection, so he moved up on her and let his cock rest between the cheeks of her buttocks. He rubbed it there until she stirred and reached behind her to take hold of him. He kissed her neck as she stroked him, then she lifted one leg so he could slide between her thighs, up and into her.

She was wet, slick, and warm, and she nestled back against him as he moved in and out of her. She groaned and moaned and, at one point, scooted away from him, expelling him momentarily so she could turn onto her back. He straddled her then slid his hands beneath her to cup her ass. She lifted her legs, and he pounded into her until he exploded with a yell . . .

The next time he woke up, there was light coming through the window, and Raquel was slipping into her skirt.

"Hey," he said.

"Good morning," she said with a smile. "I must go and work."

"Right now?"

"*Sí*," she said, straightening up. Her blouse was already on. He'd missed seeing her don it.

She came to the bed and kissed him.

"I'll be out in a few minutes," he said.

"You should sleep."

"No," he said, "my friends will be here for breakfast, and we need to talk."

"Breakfast will be ready," she promised.

After Raquel left, he washed up and put on his last clean shirt. He strapped on his gun, left the room, and walked down the hall. When he entered the cantina, he saw the three mercenaries sitting there, drinking coffee.

As he approached the table, Autry gave him a knowing look.

"What?" he asked, sitting down.

"Do I know women, or do I know women?" the big man asked.

"Shut up," Clint said, pouring himself a cup of coffee.

The other men laughed as Raquel appeared carrying trays of food. She set them down on the table, pressed her hip against Clint's shoulder, and went back to the kitchen.

"So?" Clint asked. "You find out anything from your contacts yesterday?"

The three men had decided that Autry would do the talking for them.

"We all found out the same thing," he said. "Montoya has hired Roberto Del Plata."

"And who's he?"

"Probably the best fighting man Mexico has to offer," Autry said.

"So just him?"

"No," Autry said, "he brings his own men with him, all very good."

"So now we have some professional fighting men to face as well as the Montoya family."

"Exactly," Autry said.

Piper and Harker, their mouths full, nodded their agreement.

"What about you?" Autry asked. "You said you had an idea you wanted to think about overnight?"

"That's right," Clint said. "I gave it a lot of thought last night."

"And?" Piper asked.

"I think we need to make Montoya uncomfortable," Clint said.

The three men exchanged a glance, and then Harker asked, "How do we do that?"

"We take the fight elsewhere," Clint said. "We don't let Montoya pick the place."

"And where did you have in mind?" Harker asked.

"Texas," Clint said. "If that's all right with the three of you."

"It's fine with us," Autry said.

Clint looked at Piper.

"Okay with me," the man said.

Clint studied the three men, then sat back in his chair.

"You already thought of that," he said.

"We did have a talk among ourselves along those lines," Autry said.

"Okay, then," Clint said. "Where in Texas?"

"Val Verde County," Harker said immediately.

"Why there?" Clint asked.

"We won't have to worry about law."

"Why's that?"

"The judge there is crazy," Harker said. "He holds court in a saloon called the Jersey Lily, in a town called Langtry."

"I heard of him," Autry said. "Judge Roy Bean."

"Never heard of him," Clint said, "but that sounds fine to me. The question is, how do we get Montoya there?"

"Oh," Harker said, "that part will be easy."

"How so?" Autry asked.

"He wants Clint really bad," Harker said. "That means he'll follow him . . . anywhere."

"He might even think you're runnin'," Piper said.

"Not if we all ride out together," Clint said. "If we do that, he might think we're trying to draw him out."

"So you think you'll have to ride out alone?" Harker asked.

Clint nodded and said, "Then the rest of you can come later and meet me."

"And what if he catches up to you before we do?" Piper asked.

"We'll just have to make sure that doesn't happen."

THIRTY-TWO

Inocencio Montoya gathered his family together and introduced them all to Roberto Del Plata and his men as they stood in front of his hacienda.

"These men will be aiding us as we avenge Juanito against the gringo, Clint Adams," Montoya said.

"Why do we need them, Papa?" Pablo asked.

"Because the gringo has aligned himself with other gringo mercenaries," Montoya said. "Señor Del Plata and his men will take care of them, while we—the family—take the necessary vengeance on the one they call the Gunsmith. Is this understood by everyone?"

It was understood by most. For those who did not understand, they would talk to others as they rode to Acuña.

"We ride today," he said, "now! *Andale!*"

With Inocencio Montoya at the head of the column, they rode to Acuña.

Earlier, Clint explained his plan to Rodrigo, outlining his part for the man.

"It's very simple, Rodrigo," he said. "You tell them the truth."

"The truth, *señor?*"

"That you heard us talking about going to Texas."

"But, *señor*, they will follow you."

"That's what we want, Rodrigo," Clint said. "We want them to follow us."

Montoya rode into Acuña, and the street was empty. Citizens had heard what was about to happen, and had taken to their homes and businesses, locking the doors. They were, however, at their windows, for who wanted to miss this?

"Adams!" Montoya shouted. "Clint Adams!"

Sheriff Calderon came out of his office.

"Do not get in my way, Sheriff," Montoya said.

"I am just here to watch, Señor Montoya," the sheriff said. "This is between you and Señor Adams. I would not want to miss this."

Montoya ignored the sheriff, looked over at the front of Carmelita's Cantina.

"Clint Adams! Come out."

Montoya and his men waited, their horses fidgeting.

"Del Plata," Montoya said, "with me."

"*Sí, señor.*"

They both dismounted and approached the front of the cantina with care, in case Clint Adams and his men were at the windows.

But they weren't . . .

From outside of town, Clint and the three mercenaries heard Montoya and his men before they saw them.

"Take cover," Clint said.

They dismounted, stood at the heads of their horses to keep them quiet, and watched as Montoya, his family, and his hired men went riding by, heading for Acuña.

"I didn't count, but that's a lot of men," Piper said.

"I counted twenty-five," Autry said.

"So did I," Clint said.

"We left just in time," Harker said. "In town it would've been a bloodbath."

"And the town would pay," Autry pointed out.

"Let's mount up and get to Texas," Clint said. "It won't take them long to discover we're gone from Acuña."

They mounted up and headed for the border.

Montoya and Del Plata entered the cantina. The only people inside were Rodrigo, his wife, and his sister-in-law.

"Señor Montoya," Rodrigo said. "You have come to—"

"*Silencio!*" Del Plata said, and clubbed Rodrigo to the floor with the butt of his rifle.

"Rodrigo!" Carmelita cried, rushing to her fallen husband. Raquel remained standing at the bar. Del Plata walked up to her and used the barrel of his rifle to push down the front of her blouse so that her bountiful breasts bobbed free, the dark brown nipples hard and distended.

"Del Plata!" Montoya snapped.

Del Plata turned to look at Montoya, then dropped the barrel of the rifle. Raquel's blouse stayed as it was, though, with her breasts in full view. Del Plata felt his mouth go wet. He would have to come back here.

Montoya reached down to help Rodrigo to his feet. There was a welt on his cheek from the rifle. Carmelita glared at Montoya and Del Plata.

"Where is Clint Adams?" Montoya asked.

"He is not here, *señor*," Rodrigo said.

"I can see that," Montoya said. "What I asked you is where did he go?"

"*Señor—*"

"Don't make me let Del Plata do what he wants to your sister-in-law . . . or your wife."

Del Plata looked at Carmelita. She was a pretty woman. Too big for his taste, but he wouldn't mind seeing her without her clothes. She had her sister's skin, probably had the same chocolate nipples. Yes, it would have been interesting to be in a room with both of these women, naked.

"*Hijo de puta*," Carmelita spat at Montoya.

"*Señora*," Montoya said, "I did not know my mother, so you might be correct. She might have been a whore." Turning to his hired gunman, he said, "Del Plata?"

The Mexican mercenary reached out and pinched one of Raquel's nipples hard. Her eyes widened, filled with fire, but she did not cry out.

"This one is tough, *patrón*," Del Plata said. "Let me try the other one."

Carmelita turned to face Del Plata and pulled her blouse down. Massive breasts came into view, smooth and creamy, and he had been right. She had the same dark brown nipples. She was daring him. He began to salivate.

"*Basta!*" Rodrigo said. He reached out and pulled his wife's blouse up. "I will tell you."

"You, girl!" Montoya said. "Tequila!"

Raquel did not bother to replace her blouse. With breasts still bare, she walked around behind the bar, poured two glasses of tequila, and left them on the bar. Del Plata handed Montoya one, then picked the other one up for himself. They both drank.

"Now," Montoya said to Rodrigo, "tell me."

"Texas," Rodrigo said. "He went to Texas."

"When?"

"This morning."

"Did he go alone?"

"*Sí, señor.*"

"Where are the other men?"

"Gone."

"Did you hear them say where they were going?"

"They talked," Rodrigo said. "I listened."

"And?"

"They heard that you hired Roberto Del Plata, and his

men," Rodrigo said. "They wanted Clint Adams to hire more men. He would not. They argued."

"And?"

"They left him."

Montoya turned to look at Del Plata, who shrugged.

"So he ran?" Montoya asked.

"He did not want to," Rodrigo said, "but he knew there would be many of you, and he would die."

"*Señor*," Del Plata said, still eyeing Raquel's breasts, "that would be a logical decision to make."

"For the Gunsmith?"

"For any man who wanted to live."

"You have a man who can track?"

"Of course."

Montoya looked at Rodrigo.

"If I find out you are lying, I will come back, burn down your place, and let Del Plata and his men have your women."

Rodrigo drew himself up to his full height and said, "I would kill them first, *señor*."

Montoya eyed Rodrigo, and then said, "*Sí*, I believe you would."

"He is a brave little man, *patrón*," Del Plata said. "Shall I kill him?"

"No!" Carmelita yelled.

Montoya thought a moment, then said, "No. Leave him."

Montoya left.

Del Plata looked at Raquel, said, "Another time, *chica*," and followed his boss.

THIRTY-THREE

Montoya and his men waited at the north end of Acuña for Del Plata and his tracker. When they returned, he, Francisco, and Pablo rode out to meet them.

"What did you find?"

"Tell him, Victorio."

The tracker, in his forties with a lot of miles on him, said, "One man left town alone, heading north."

"The other three?"

"Left town together, then split up," Victorio explained. "One headed for Texas, the others look like they are staying here, in Mexico."

"Piper and Autry live in Mexico, *patrón*," Del Plata said. "Harker lives in Texas."

"So . . . they went home?"

"That is what it looks like."

Montoya chewed his bottom lip.

"Do you want us to check and see if they all really went home?" Del Plata asked.

"No," Montoya said, "that will give Clint Adams too big a head start."

"So that means . . . we are going after Clint Adams?" Del Plata asked.

"We are."

"All of us?"

Montoya pointed at Victorio and said, "All of us . . . except him."

"*Patrón?*" Victorio said, frowning.

"I want you to go to the cantina and check where Clint Adams kept his horse," Montoya instructed. "I want to make sure those tracks are his."

"*Sí, sí, patrón,*" Victorio said. "I will go and do that right away."

"Then catch up to us."

"*Sí.*"

Victorio wheeled his horse around and rode back into Acuña at a gallop.

Montoya looked at Del Plata.

"We are riding to Texas . . . now!"

They rode for a couple of hours before Victorio caught up to them.

"*Patrón!*" he called.

Montoya reined in and waited. Victorio caught up to them, reined in his own horse between Montoya and Del Plata.

"Well?" Montoya asked.

"I checked the tracks, *patrón,*" Victorio said. "They are the same."

"Are we still following the right trail?"

Victorio looked at the ground ahead of them and said, "*Sí, patrón.*"

"Very well," Montoya said, "then take the point, Victorio."

"*Sí, señor.*"

Clint rode into Langtry, Texas, which was in Val Verde County, about eighty miles from Acuña. He, Piper, Autry, and Harker had agreed to meet there, a decent enough distance away from Acuña so that Montoya might lose some of his men along the way. Also, at this distance Montoya would assume he was running.

Langtry was small, just a few buildings, and they looked like they were falling down. If he had to face Montoya and his men here, it wouldn't do all that much damage. He had to steer Eclipse around a bunch of chickens as he entered town.

The surprising thing, however, was that the town had a railroad station.

He rode up to the Jersey Lily Saloon, and dismounted. He had ridden directly from Acuña, and it was almost dark. He needed a drink, and some food, and hoped he could get both inside.

As he entered, the three men there turned to look at him. Two of them turned away and went back to their drinking; the third man was the bartender. He watched as Clint approached the bar.

"Beer," Clint said.

"Comin' up."

He looked down at the bar, saw some round circles in it, as if someone had been banging on it with a hammer . . . or a gavel.

"Here ya go," the bartender said. He saw Clint looking at the bar. "That's from the judge's gavel."

"Judge."

"Judge Roy Bean," the man said.

"Ah."

"Heard of him?"

"I think so." Clint sipped his beer. "Just recently. Somebody mentioned him."

"Well," the man said, "stay out of trouble and you won't have to meet 'im."

"I always plan to stay out of trouble," Clint said. "Any chance of getting something to eat?"

"Sandwich maybe," the man said. "Some hard-boiled eggs?"

"That'll do."

"Comin' up."

"Thanks."

Clint turned with his beer and looked the saloon over. It was newer than the other buildings in town. But the furniture, and the bar, were not new.

Over the bar was a painting Clint recognized.

Lily Langtry, the actress. He had run into her a few times, the last time in New York.

"This town named for her?" he asked the bartender when he brought out a small bowl of hard-boiled eggs.

"Nope," the bartender said, "some other fella named Langtry. But the saloon is. I'll get you that sandwich. Start on the eggs."

"Thanks."

Clint peeled three eggs, began eating them, and washed them down with the beer. By the time the bartender came back with the sandwich, he had finished all three.

"Chicken," the man said. "That's all I had."

"That's fine."

"Eat it," the bartender said. "Then the judge wants to talk to you."

"Talk to me?" Clint asked, accepting the sandwich. "But . . . why?"

The bartender shrugged.

"Who knows why the judge does anything?" he said. "Maybe he saw you ride in and recognized you."

"Recognized me?"

"Well, he said you were Clint Adams, the Gunsmith." The bartender waited, and when Clint said nothing, he asked, "You are Clint Adams, aren't you?"

Clint bit into the sandwich and said, "I guess he recognized me, then. Where is he?"

"That door in the back," the bartender said. "I'll get you another beer. When you're finished eating, just knock."

"I'll do that. Thanks."

THIRTY-FOUR

Clint finished the sandwich, washed it down with the beer, then walked to the door the bartender had indicated and knocked.

"Come!"

He opened the door and entered. A white-haired man with a surprisingly unlined face was seated behind a desk. He was in shirtsleeves, with suspenders and—oddly—was wearing a stovepipe hat indoors. He had a pair of wire-framed glasses perched on the end of his nose.

"Judge?"

"That's me," the man said. "Roy Bean. Come on in, Mr. Adams. Close the door. Have a seat. Get enough to eat?"

"Actually, no," Clint said, "but I suppose it will have to do."

"I have a woman who makes me soup," the judge said. "You interested?"

"What kind?"

"Does that matter?"

"Actually, no."

"Good. Have a seat, then."

Clint sat across from the man.

"How did you know who I am?"

"I saw you ride in," Bean said.

"Yes, but how did you recognize me?"

"I saw you in Fort Smith once," Bean said. "I was visiting a friend."

"A friend?"

"Judge Isaac Parker."

"Ah."

"You know Judge Parker?"

"Very well."

"Hm," Judge Bean said, "then that means you don't like him."

"Not much."

"But you respect him?"

"A great deal."

"Good," Bean said. "Now, suppose you tell me what brings you to Langtry."

"Is that your business?"

"Oh yes," Bean said, "it is very much my business. This is my town, my county. If you're bringing trouble to it, I'd like to know about it."

"Do you have a lawman?"

"We have a man who wears a badge," Bean said. "That's as close as we come."

"Ah."

"So," Bean said, "my question."

"What I'm doing here?"

"Yes," Bean said, "and I'd really appreciate the truth."

Clint decided to tell him.

Roy Bean listened to the story intently, then sat quietly for a few moments after Clint had finished.

"Guess you don't think much of Langtry, do you, Mr. Adams?" he asked then.

"I didn't know anything about it, Judge."

"Well, it may not look like much, but it's home to some people," Bean said. "They won't appreciate you gettin' it all shot up."

"I'll try not to," Clint said. "My intention is simply to meet my men here. When we engage Montoya and his men, it won't be in your town."

"You guarantee that?"

"I guarantee that I'll try to keep it from happening. You don't have a hotel, do you?"

"We do, but I doubt you and your men will be welcome there," Bean said.

"No problem," Clint said. "We'll camp away from town."

"You know," Bean said, "if this darned battle of yours takes place in my jurisdiction, you're gonna end up in my court."

"Well, if that happens, Judge," Clint said, "I hope you'll be lenient with me if I survive, and hard on Montoya if he does."

"My gavel only swings one way, Mr. Adams."

"Call me Clint."

"That's fine," Bean said, "and you can call me Judge."

"I wouldn't have it any other way."

"Fine," Bean said, standing up. "Let's go and have that soup."

THIRTY-FIVE

Clint did not meet the woman who cooked for Judge Roy Bean, but he did get to taste her chicken soup.

"We got chickens all over the place," Bean said. "They're the easiest things to take care of."

"That explains why I got hard-boiled eggs and a chicken sandwich from the bartender."

"Ain't had a steak in a coon's age," Bean said. "Every once in a while I ride up to Fort Stockton to get one, but it's been a while."

They were sitting at a back table in the Jersey Lily, as the soup was usually brought to the judge there. They were drinking beer brought to them by the bartender.

"When do you expect the rest of your men?" the judge asked.

"Shortly," Clint said. "I had to leave first to give the impression I was running."

"You think anybody's gonna believe that the Gunsmith ran from a fight?"

"Against twenty-five men? Why not?"

Judge Bean shrugged.

"Don't sit right with me, is all," he said. "Seems to me runnin' don't come easy to some men."

"Remember," Clint said, "I'm not really running."

"So you say."

Clint had the feeling Judge Bean was trying to get his goat, and he wasn't biting. The man may have just been testing him, for some reasons of his own.

"I'm aware of Inocencio Montoya," Bean said. "Sounds like the kind of man I'd like to get in my court."

"Now that's something I'd like to see," Clint said. "I have the feeling there's no court in Mexico that he's ever seen the inside of."

"Well, this ain't Mexico," Bean said. "This is Val Verde County. I rule here."

They finished their soup and Clint said, "The bartender told me this town wasn't named for Lily Langtry."

"That's true," Bean said. "It was named for George, who built the railroad."

"It seems to me that a town with a railroad station would be bigger."

"We're growin'," Bean said. "Was a time the Jersey Lily was just a tent. And a few years ago, we were made the post office for the county."

"Are you the postmaster?"

"Not me," Bean said. "I got enough to do bein' the justice of the peace, the notary public, and the Law West of the Pecos. Speakin' of which," he said, standing up, "I got work to do. Why don't you have another beer and wait for your friends."

"My guess is they'll arrive tomorrow morning," Clint said. "What do you say to a hotel room, just for tonight?"

Roy Bean scowled, but said, "Yeah, okay. End of the street. Tell Wendell I said it was okay."

"Thanks, Judge."

"Better not be no trouble, though," Bean said. "You see how nice I can be. You don't wanna see my other side."

"No, Judge," Clint said, "I sure don't."

* * *

Clint walked his horse to the hotel and relayed the message to the desk clerk, Wendell, a sleepy-looking man in his sixties. He signed Clint in, gave him a key, and told him where the livery stable was.

As he walked down the street, Clint realized that Langtry was larger than he'd first thought. It was more than the few buildings he'd seen riding in, as it then spread out some.

He found the livery, turned Eclipse over to an impressed-looking man in his fifties.

"This is some horse," the man said.

"Treat him that way," Clint said.

"Don't worry, mister," the liveryman said. "I'll take care of 'im."

Clint collected his saddlebags and rifle and walked back to the hotel.

In his room he stared out the window, wondered if there was any chance that Montoya would forget about his vengeance once he realized Clint was gone. That was probably too much to ask.

He walked to the bed and sat on it. The mattress was like sleeping on the ground. A town with a railroad station ought to have a better hotel.

After a while he decided to go back to the Jersey Lily for a beer.

He was drinking his beer, looking up at the portrait of Lily Langtry, when he said to the bartender, "You know, that's not even a good likeness of her."

The man laughed and said, "How would you know?"

"I know her," Clint said. "Met her a few times. In fact, I spent some time with her in New York. She's a very nice lady."

The bartender had been staring at him with his mouth open after he spoke the first three words, "I know her."

"You met Lily Langtry?"

"That's right."

"I mean," the bartender went on, "you actually met her, and talked to her. You didn't just see her onstage."

"I met her and talked to her." Clint didn't tell him what else he'd done with Lily.

"Did you tell this to the judge?"

"I didn't."

"Oh, my God," the bartender said. "If you do, he'll never let you leave."

"Interesting," Clint said. "So if I tell him, I'll be able to keep my hotel room longer?"

"Probably."

"And he won't make me leave?"

"I don't think so."

Clint hesitated, then said, "I don't think I should tell him."

"Why not?"

"He might think I'm lying," Clint said. "But if you tell him . . ."

"What if you are lying?" the bartender said.

"Hmm? Why would I?"

"To get me to tell the judge that you know her."

Clint shrugged.

"Don't tell him, then."

"I can't do that," the bartender said. "If he ever found out . . ."

"It's up to you, then," Clint said. "Bring me another beer while you're trying to make up your mind, will you?"

"Sure."

The bartender set a fresh beer in front of him, and then disappeared.

THIRTY-SIX

Clint was in his room, sitting on the hard bed, reading, when somebody knocked on his door. He grabbed his gun and walked to it.

"Who is it?"

"Judge Roy Bean."

He opened the door.

The judge held out a bottle of whiskey.

"Tell me," he said, "all about it."

They sat up all night, drinking the whiskey, talking about Lily Langtry. Clint told him almost everything he knew about her—except how she looked naked. But Roy Bean didn't want to know that. He worshiped her like a goddess, so he'd never want to hear anything like that.

So Clint told him everything else he knew about the dear lady, and then made up some things. By the time the sun came up, he knew he'd be able to keep that hotel room for as long as he wanted.

Roy Bean looked at the window and said, "It's morning."

"Yes."

"We both need some sleep," the judge said. "Come to the Jersey Lily in a few hours and we'll have breakfast."

The judge stood up.

"But . . . I have to check out."

The judge walked to the door, turned, and said, "Don't be an ass."

Clint went to the Jersey Lily for a late breakfast with the judge.

But before that, still several hours away, Piper poured coffee for himself, Harker, and Autry.

"We could have kept going," he said. "We'd be eating breakfast right now."

"And one of our horses would have a broken leg," Autry said. "It's just as well we camped. We'll be there before noon, and we can have lunch."

"How far behind us do you think Montoya and his men are?" Piper asked.

"Depends," Harker said.

"On what?" Piper asked.

"Whether or not they rode to my house to see if I really went home."

"If they did that," Autry said, "and they saw you weren't there, they'd figure it out. That we didn't really split up."

"They might," Harker said. "It's more likely they're tracking Clint, following his trail."

"Which he's not trying to hide at all," Piper pointed out.

"Let's hope he's not being too obvious about it," Autry said.

"What do you think?" Piper asked.

Clint and Judge Roy Bean had a full ham-and-eggs breakfast, complete with fresh buttered biscuits and potatoes.

"Are you a steak-and-eggs man?" the judge asked while they ate.

"I am," Clint said. "It's my preferred breakfast."

"Well, you'll have it tomorrow morning," Bean assured him.

"I thought you had to go to Fort Stockton for steak," Clint asked.

"I'm havin' it brought in," Bean said.

The night before, in his room, Bean had told Clint how many times he had seen Lily Langtry perform. He also told him how many times he had almost spoken to the Jersey Lily, only to back down.

"I don't mind admittin'," Judge Roy Bean had said, "I was scared."

So, as someone who was afraid to speak to the woman he worshiped, the fact that Clint knew her—and he had told Bean enough about her to convince him that he was telling the truth—went a long way toward making him welcome in Langtry, no matter who was on his trail.

"I appreciate that, Judge," Clint said, "but I still don't intend to bring a firefight into your town."

"If Inocencio Montoya tries to take you in Langtry," Judge Roy Bean said, "I'll throw his aristocratic ass into my jail."

"I'd like to see that," Clint admitted.

At that moment the batwings of the Jersey Lily opened and three men walked in.

"Yours?" the judge asked.

Clint nodded and said, "Mine."

THIRTY-SEVEN

Clint waved Piper, Autry, and Harker over and introduced them to Judge Roy Bean.

Harker—the only one of them who had ever heard of the judge—said, "A pleasure, your honor."

Piper and Autry were looking at the remnants of the meal on the table.

"Would you gents like some food?" the judge asked.

"Oh, yes, your honor, we would," Piper said.

"Grab a table," Bean said. "I'll have my man bring you some ham and eggs."

"Thanks, Judge," Clint said.

Bean nodded and went to the kitchen. The three mercenaries grabbed a table and Clint joined them.

"Any sign of Montoya and his men?" he asked them.

"No," Harker said, "not yet anyway. But we knew where we were headin', and they're trackin' you. We probably just traveled faster than they did."

The bartender came with coffee and poured for all four of them. There were no other customers in the saloon. Clint nodded his thanks to the man.

"They should be here sometime today," Harker said. "Unless they get lost."

"Not much chance of that," Piper said.

"What's the plan?" Autry asked.

"Well," Clint said, "I did have some ideas, but things have changed a bit."

"How so?" Autry asked.

"We suddenly have the Law West of the Pecos on our side," he explained.

"The judge?" Harker asked.

Clint nodded.

"How'd you manage that?"

"I didn't," Clint said. "Lily Langtry did."

In the kitchen Roy Bean said to the bartender, "Get ahold of Leroy."

"Sir?"

"I want him to ride out and watch for riders," Bean said. "I want to know when those Mexicans are comin'."

"Yes, sir."

The table was covered with food within a few minutes, and the three mercenaries dug in.

"Been a long time since I had me an American breakfast," Piper commented.

"Me, too," Autry said.

"That's what you get for livin' in Mexico," Harker said with a big smile. "I eat like this all the time."

"If I ate like this all the time," Piper said, "my horse wouldn't be able to carry me."

Harker slapped his stomach and said happily, "I never put on weight."

"You're lucky," Autry said. "With my size, I can easily get to three hundred pounds."

They all looked at him.

"Well, not now," Autry said.

"What's your new plan?" Harker asked.

"Judge Bean isn't happy about Mexicans crossing into Texas and coming to his county," Clint said.

"Did you tell him they're not about to care what the law thinks?" Piper asked.

"Especially Del Plata and his men," Autry added.

"Well," Clint said, "the judge seems to think he can handle anything with his gavel."

"The way I hear it," Harker said, "he pretty much can."

"Then I'll talk to him," Clint said, "and see what he has to say."

"Ain't you gonna eat somethin'?" Piper asked. "It's almost all gone."

"Well, I, uh—" Clint said, looking at the remains of the eggs and ham and biscuits. "Oh, what the hell. I'm not worried about gaining weight."

THIRTY-EIGHT

Later that afternoon Montoya reined in his horse and pointed ahead at Victorio.

"Victorio!" Del Plata shouted.

The tracker stopped, turned, and then rode back to them.

"That town up ahead," Montoya said. "What is it called?"

"Langtry, *patrón*."

"Have you ever been there?"

"No."

"Has anyone ever been there?" Montoya called out.

No one had.

"What do you want to do, *señor?*" Del Plata asked.

"I want you to send your man ahead to have a look at the town," Montoya said. "I want to know if it has any law, how big it is . . . and if Clint Adams is there."

"*Sí, patrón*," Del Plata said. "Perhaps I should go with him?"

"No," Montoya said, "just one man. I do not want any undue attention."

Del Plata nodded, and looked at Victorio.

"Did you hear?"

"*Sí, Jefe.*"

"Then go and do it," Del Plata ordered. "Come right back here with what you find out."

"Sí, Jefe."

Victorio rode on toward Langtry.

Clint was sitting with Piper, Autry, and Harker when a skinny man came running into the saloon.

"Where's the judge?" he asked the bartender.

"In his office."

The man ran to the judge's door and opened it without knocking.

"They're here!" he yelled.

Clint got up and walked to the opened door, looked in. The man was standing before the judge's desk.

"How many?" the judge asked.

"A lot," Leroy said, "but they're sending one man ahead."

"To scout," Clint said.

Judge Bean looked past Leroy to Clint.

"They'll want to make sure I'm here," Clint said, "and that I'm alone."

"We can show them that," the judge said.

"Maybe if I leave—"

"No," Bean said, "that won't be necessary. We can show them what they want to see."

"They'll also be checking on how many men you have."

Judge Bean stood up.

"We can handle that, too. You can go, Leroy."

"You want me to do anything else, Judge?"

"Just tell the men to be on call."

"Okay."

Leroy turned and rushed past Clint.

"The men?"

"You'll see when the time comes," Judge Bean said. "For now we'd better get your men out of sight."

When Victorio entered the Jersey Lily, Clint was sitting at a table alone. The only other person in the saloon was the bartender.

The Mexican went to the bar and said, "*Cerveza, por favor.*"

"Sure thing."

The bartender set a beer on the bar.

"Quiet town," Victorio said.

"Very quiet."

Victorio drank some beer, risked a look over his shoulder at Clint, who pretended not to notice. He seemed to be concentrating on the beer mug in front of him.

"You do not have much crime, then?" Victorio asked.

"No crime," the bartender said, "no law."

"No *jefe?* Uh, sheriff?"

The bartender shrugged.

"We don't need one."

"That . . . is very good for you."

"Yeah, it is."

Victorio drank down his beer, paid for it, and left the saloon.

Judge Bean came out of his office.

"So now we wait," he said.

"We wait," Clint agreed.

"Come with me," Bean said to Clint. "I want to show you something."

Outside the saloon, Victorio looked around. There was no one on the streets. It was quiet. Almost dead.

Langtry seemed to be a ghost town.

He mounted his horse and rode out.

Montoya and the rest were right where he left them.

"No law, *patrón,*" Victorio said. "It does not even look like there are any people. It is like a . . . a ghost town."

"What did you see exactly?" Montoya asked.

"Just a bartender in a saloon."

"Any customers?"

"One."

"What did he look like?"

Victorio told them.

"It is him," Montoya said.

"Are you sure, *patrón?*" Del Plata asked.

"Well," Montoya said, "we are going to ride into Langtry and find out."

THIRTY-NINE

"They're comin' in," Leroy said. "All of 'em."

"All right, Leroy," Judge Bean said. "Take your position."

"Yes, sir."

He left the Jersey Lily, carrying his rifle.

"Are you sure you have enough?" Clint asked.

"It's not how many," Bean said. "It's all in the positioning. Speaking of which . . ."

"I should get into position, too."

"Yes."

"Look, Judge—"

"Don't," Judge Roy Bean said. "Any friend of Lily Langtry's is a friend of mine."

"Yes, sir."

Clint went out.

Montoya and his men rode into Langtry. Immediately, they saw what Victorio had seen—empty streets, a quiet little town. There was also a man sitting in a chair in front of the Jersey Lily.

"That's him," Montoya said. "That's Clint Adams."

"So," Del Plata said, "that is the famous Gunsmith."

"*Sí.*"

"How do you want to do this?"

"I want him dead," Montoya said, "and I want to pull the trigger."

"Well then, *señor*," Del Plata said, "unless you want to do it from here with a rifle, we better get closer." Del Plata turned to his men. "No one fires unless the *patrón* does. *Comprende?*"

Not only did his men nod, but the rest did as well.

Clint watched as the large group of riders—easily twenty-five, so they hadn't lost any during the ride—approached him. He supposed he should have been flattered.

The only way they were able to all stand in front of the saloon was by gathering in the center of the street. Front and center, though, were Inocencio Montoya and his Mexican mercenary, Roberto Del Plata.

"Adams," Montoya said. "You didn't run very far."

"I didn't run at all, Montoya," Clint said. "Here I am."

"Alone?" Montoya asked. "Where are your paid killers? Did they desert you?"

"Not at all," Clint said. He had one foot planted against a wooden post, was leaning back slightly, but he had his gun clear for a quick grab, if it came to that. "They're around."

Montoya couldn't control his eyes. He looked around, didn't see any of the American mercenaries.

Montoya brought his eyes back to Clint, who was seemingly unconcerned.

"I told you what was going to happen to you for shooting my son," Montoya said.

"Yes, you did," Clint replied. "You said I'd have to face you and your family. Looks like your family got a little bigger since then."

"You are a professional gunman," Montoya said, "and you did warn me that I would lose some family members if I came after you."

"And you will," Clint said, "but first you'll lose your own

life, Montoya, because you're the first one I'll kill. Even if I only get one of you, it will be you."

Montoya didn't like that, but he stood his ground. Del Plata was giving Clint a good, long, hard study.

"Stand up," Montoya said. "The time has come."

"Here?" Clint asked. "In town? This town has done nothing to you. Why would you shoot it up?"

"You chose this town, Adams," Montoya said, "I did not."

"You're right, Montoya," Clint said, "I did choose the place . . . and perhaps you should think about that. We're not in Mexico now, where the law doesn't apply to you."

"What does it matter?" Montoya asked. "There is no law here."

"But there is," Clint said.

Montoya turned his head to look directly at Del Plata's man, Victorio.

"In fact, allow me to introduce you to the local law—in fact, the Law West of the Pecos—Judge Roy Bean."

Roy Bean stepped out from between the Jersey Lily batwings and stood next to Clint. He was still in shirtsleeves and suspenders, wearing his stovepipe hat, with a slim cigar sticking out of his mouth. He was also wearing a pistol in a holster.

"Señor Montoya."

"You are a judge?" Montoya asked in disbelief.

"I sure am." Bean took something from his belt. "In fact, here's my gavel. See?" He held the gavel up.

"That means nothing," Montoya said.

"Well," Bean said, "maybe you'll take the word of our sheriff?"

The batwings opened again and a man wearing a badge stepped out. Clint had been surprised when Roy Bean told him that the bartender was not only his bailiff, but the sheriff of Langtry as well.

"Sheriff Benson," Roy Bean said, "meet Señor Montoya."

The sheriff simply nodded. He was holding a rifle in his hands.

Montoya turned to Del Plata and said something in Spanish. Clint thought he must have been complaining that he thought there was no law in Langtry.

So now there were three men standing against the twenty-five Mexicans.

Now," Roy Bean said, "we ain't gonna take too kindly to it if you shoot up our town."

"Then we will take Adams with us," Montoya said, "and kill him outside your town."

"Ah, but you'll still be in my county," Bean said. "Also wouldn't take kindly to murder in my county."

Montoya started to do a slow burn.

"Then we will take him back to Mexico."

"I can't allow that," Bean said.

"Why not?"

"Mr. Adams is my guest."

Montoya leaned forward in his saddle and said, "Then we will kill him, and burn your town down around your ears . . . Judge."

"Naw," Bean said, "I don't think yer gonna do that."

"Why not?"

This time the sheriff spoke up.

"Meet my deputies."

Suddenly, gun barrels appeared from doorways, windows, and rooftops. Montoya could hear live rounds being levered into them. Clint thought that Judge Roy Bean must have deputized the entire town population.

"You're covered from all angles, *señor*," Benson said. "You try anything and a lot of your family ain't gonna be goin' home."

"Your move," Clint said.

Del Plata turned to Montoya and said, "We can do it, *patrón*. We still have numbers on our side."

"You are a fool," Montoya said. "They have position. They would cut half of us down before we could get our guns out."

"*Señor*," Del Plata said, "my men will fight."

"And die," Montoya said.

"So what do we do?" Del Plata asked.

"I don't know," Montoya said, "yet."

FORTY

"What are you thinkin', Señor Montoya?" Judge Roy Bean asked.

"I am thinking that you have some sort of bargain to make, *señor*," Montoya said.

Bean laughed.

"I might at that."

"What do you propose?"

"Well, first I propose that you turn and ride out and forget all about Clint Adams."

"That I cannot do, *señor*."

"No," Bean said, "I didn't think you'd agree to that. Well, then, I suggest you dismount and come into my court."

"Am I on trial?"

"No," Bean said, "but I don't only hold trials in my court. I also mediate disagreements."

"Mediate?"

"I listen to both sides of a disagreement, and then I propose a way for both parties to be satisfied."

"Ah, I see."

"So, I invite you and Clint Adams into my court." Bean indicated the batwing doors behind him. "Whataya say?"

Montoya leaned over to talk first to his brother, Francisco, and then to Del Plata.

"I agree," Montoya said, "but I would like to bring two men with me."

"Not a problem," Judge Roy Bean said. "Dismount."

Montoya began to dismount when Del Plata grabbed his arm, stopping him. He leaned over and said something into the man's ear. Montoya nodded his understanding, or his agreement.

"Judge, we will not give up our weapons."

"Not a problem," Bean said, "neither will we. If you want to start something inside, it'll end in a bloodbath."

"We only wish to be able to defend ourselves," Montoya explained.

"Well," Bean said, "nobody could argue with that, could they?"

"No, *señor.*"

Montoya, his brother, and Roberto Del Plata all dismounted. They handed the reins of their horses to other men. Clint noticed that Montoya handed his reins not to his son, but to another man, possibly his foreman.

As the three men mounted the boardwalk, Clint stood up from his chair.

"Gentlemen," Roy Bean said, allowing the three Mexicans to enter.

"*Señor,*" Montoya said, waving Bean to go first.

"Ah, you're suspicious," Bean said. "You think I have a bunch of guns inside?"

"I am just being careful, *señor,*" Montoya said. "No one could blame me for that, eh?"

"Nope," Bean said, "nobody could."

He entered the saloon first, confidently, and was followed by the three Mexicans, who were in turn followed by Sheriff Benson and Clint Adams.

The man Montoya had handed his reins to was, indeed, his foreman, Enrique Mejías.

Montoya's son, Pablo, leaned over and said, "We should do something."

"What do you suggest?" Mejías asked.

Pablo looked around, said, "We outnumber them, and the Gunsmith is inside."

"*Sí*," Mejías said, "and so is your father. At the first sound of a shot, Adams will kill him."

"He has Del Plata with him."

"Del Plata is no match for the Gunsmith."

"Truly?" Pablo asked. "You believe that?"

"I do."

"Then what do you suggest we should do?"

Mejías looked around at all the guns that were pointed at them, then turned and looked at his own men before leaning over and replying to Pablo.

"We do exactly what the *patrón* told us to do," he said. "We wait."

"But, Mejías—"

"We wait!" Mejías said again.

FORTY-ONE

Inside the Jersey Lily, Montoya saw there was no one else present.

Judge Roy Bean went around behind the bar, raised his gavel, and brought it down on the bar.

"Court's in session!" Sheriff Benson said in his capacity as bailiff. "The honorable Judge Roy Bean presiding."

"Mr. Adams, will you sit there, please?" Judge Bean said, pointing. "And Señor Montoya, you and your men there. Thank you."

From the look on Montoya's face, Clint thought he was finally starting to believe that this was a real court. He sat at a table with his men, and removed his hat. Tentatively, his brother and mercenary also removed theirs.

Sheriff Benson took up position on the outside of the bar, his rifle held ready.

"Now then," Judge Bean said. "Señor Montoya, you are the one who has a grudge against Mr. Adams. Suppose you tell the court what happened?"

"It is very simple," Montoya said. "Clint Adams shot my oldest son, Juanito."

"I'm afraid I'm gonna need some more details from you,

señor," the judge said from around his cigar. Clint could see that the man was enjoying himself. He loved holding court.

"It is simple," Montoya said. "Clint Adams is a professional gunman, and he shot down an innocent boy."

"Innocent boy?" Clint said. "What the hell—"

Judge Bean slammed his gavel down, cutting Clint off.

"You'll have your chance to speak, Mr. Adams," Bean said. "Don't make me hold you in contempt."

"Sorry, Judge."

"Go on, Señor Montoya."

"I have no more to say."

"Why did Adams shoot your son?"

"I do not know," Montoya said. "And it does not matter."

"Well, it matters to the court," Bean said. "What was your son doin'?"

"I was not there."

"Where did it happen?"

"In the livery stable."

"Was there a witness?"

"Not to the actual shooting, no. But my son told me—"

Bean slammed his gavel down.

"I can't listen to you tell me what your son said," he announced. "It's hearsay. Is your son here to testify?"

"Of course not."

Bean slammed his gavel down.

"Enough!" he said. "Mr. Adams? Tell me your side."

"Well, Judge, I was there, so there's nothing hearsay about this," Clint said. "That boy pushed me, and he wouldn't back down. He tried it earlier, in a cantina, but his father stopped him. But when he cornered me in the livery stable, his father wasn't there. Just him. He wanted to try me, and he didn't give me a choice."

"But you didn't kill him."

"No, sir, I did not."

"Why not?"

"I didn't have to."

"A man drew on you and yon didn't have to kill him?"

"He wasn't half as good with a gun as he thought he was," Clint said.

"I see." Judge Bean looked at Montoya. "How is your son, Señor Montoya?"

"He is recovering."

"He's in no danger of dying?"

"No."

"Then I don't see the problem, *señor*," the judge said. "It sounds to me like you owe Mr. Adams a debt of gratitude for not killing your son."

"I did thank Mr. Adams for not killing my son," Montoya said.

"But you still want to kill him."

"Yes."

"Why?"

"He must pay."

"I don't understand."

"I have a reputation to protect," Montoya said. "I cannot have such a thing go unpunished."

"Then I suggest you punish your son," Roy Bean said. "Seems he was the one who did something stupid."

"We are not in Mexico," Montoya said, "or you would understand."

"No, we are not in Mexico," Bean said. "If you want to kill Clint Adams and get away with it, you'll have to wait until he once again goes to Mexico. It's not gonna happen in my county. Or in Texas. Understand?"

"This is ridiculous!" Montoya said, jumping to his feet.

Sheriff Benson immediately pointed his rifle at Montoya. Del Plata reached out to stay his employer's hand. Montoya did not move.

Judge Bean slammed his gavel down repeatedly on the poor, scarred bar top.

"It's time for you to get out of my court, Señor Montoya,"

the judge said, "out of my town, out of my county, and out of Texas. If any harm comes to Clint Adams in Texas, you'll have to deal with the Texas Rangers."

"May I speak?" Roberto Del Plata asked.

"Who are you?"

He stood.

"My name is Roberto Del Plata. I work for Señor Montoya."

"As what?" Judge Bean asked.

"Um . . . well, in your language you would say I am a . . . fighting man."

"And what do you have to say?"

"I have a suggestion."

"And what's that?"

"Mr. Adams has some professional guns working for him," Del Plata said, "and Señor Montoya does also."

"The court stipulates to that fact," Bean said. "What is your suggestion?"

"I suggest that his gunmen and Señor Montoya's gunmen solve this on the street."

"How many such men do you have?" Bean asked.

"Counting me, six."

"And you?" Bean asked Clint.

"Counting me, five."

"Seems almost fair," Bean said. "Señor Montoya? Would you abide by such an arrangement?"

"No."

"No? Why not?"

"Someone from my family must be involved."

"So . . . you want your own son to take part in this . . . this duel?"

"No," Montoya said, "my brother." He pointed to Francisco.

"And you go along with this?" Judge Bean asked.

Francisco looked at his brother, then at the judge, and said, "*Sí*, Judge."

"Well," Bean said, "I'll have to take this under advisement. If you'll all wait outside, I'll call you in when I've made a decision."

They all seemed somewhat confused by that so Sheriff Benson said, "Court's adjourned for ten minutes. Wait outside!"

FORTY-TWO

When they went outside, Montoya, his brother, and Del Plata went and joined their men in the street. Clint found Harker standing on the boardwalk in front of the saloon.

"What's goin' on?" Harker asked.

"The judge is going to rule."

"On what?"

"We'll find out."

"You think Montoya will go by his ruling?"

"No. Where are Piper and Autry?"

"On the roof."

"What about all these other guns?"

"You don't wanna know," Harker said. "Those two across the street, in that window? Two little girls."

"Christ," Clint said.

"If they start shooting," Harker said, "we're gonna get these people slaughtered."

"Well," Clint said, "Bean did come up with an idea . . ." Clint told Harker about it.

"That'd be five against seven," Harker said. "Would you accept that?"

"It's better than five against twenty-five," Clint pointed out. "And it's better than getting these people killed."

"I suppose," Harker said, "but where would this show-down take place?"

"Maybe the judge will have a suggestion about that, too."

"Let's hope . . ."

Sheriff Benson came out ten minutes later.

"The judge is ready," he called.

They filed back into the saloon, Del Plata bringing up the rear. They sat back down in their chairs.

"Here's my ruling," Bean said. "Mr. Adams had no choice but to do what he did. You owe him your son's life, because he could have killed him very easily. You've got no reason to want to kill him."

"You said you have a ruling," Montoya said. "You also said this was a . . . what did you call it?"

"Mediation," Benson said.

"*Sí*, a mediation," Montoya said. "That means you do not rule, you suggest a solution. Correct?"

"Technically correct," Bean said.

"Technically?"

"Like I said," Bean told him, "my town, my country, I'm the law. So I'm gonna rule."

"You cannot—"

Judge Bean slammed his gavel down.

"You will quiet down or I'll throw you in a cell for contempt," he barked.

Montoya subsided, but he was livid.

"You and your men will go back to Mexico," Bean said. "If you don't, I'll call in the Texas Rangers."

"You cannot do that," Montoya said. "You do not have enough time."

"On the contrary, *señor*. They are already on standby," Bean said. "During the last ten minutes I sent them a telegraph message. If they don't hear from me again in fifteen minutes, they'll be on their way."

Montoya pointed outside.

"My men can reduce this town to ashes before then!" Montoya hissed.

"Try it!" Bean said. "It'll burn to the ground with you in my jail cell."

Don Inocencio Montoya stood up, and his body shook with rage. He clenched his fists at his sides. Del Plata and Francisco stood up next to him.

Sheriff Benson pointed his rifle at them, and Judge Roy Bean was seconds away from drawing his own gun.

Clint stood, as well. They could probably end it all here and now. But when the shots were heard outside, who knew what could happen?

"No," Clint said, "wait."

The other men in the saloon looked at him.

"What is it, Mr. Adams?" Judge Bean asked.

Clint looked at all four men in turn, and then said, "I think I have a better idea."

FORTY-THREE

Montoya led Francisco and Roberto Del Plata to their horses. They mounted up, and then all twenty-five Mexicans rode out.

When Piper, Autry, and Harker came walking in, Clint was at the bar, drinking a beer with Judge Roy Bean. Sheriff/Bailiff Benson was back behind the bar in his capacity as bartender.

"Beers?" he asked.

"Yeah," Harker said, "all around."

"What happened?" Piper asked.

"They just . . . left."

"Oh, they're not gone," Clint said. "They're . . . waiting."

"Are you sure about this?" Judge Bean asked him.

"Sure as I can be that I don't want this town and the people in it to pay a high price for backing me," Clint said.

"I *can* get the Texas Rangers here," Bean said. "I may have lied about already contacting them, but I can get them here."

"No," Clint said. "This is personal. No point in getting the whole state of Texas involved."

"What's going on?" Piper asked.

"We're back where we started," Clint said. "Us against

them. Or me against them. I don't expect you fellas to ride into a hailstorm of lead for me."

"Hey," Autry said, "the whole point was that we would be riding into a hailstorm of lead with you, the Gunsmith." He raised his beer. "Make us all famous, right?"

"I don't know about that," Clint said, "but it could make us all dead."

Outside of Langtry, Montoya reined in his horse, turned to look at his family and his employees. Quickly, he explained what had happened in Judge Roy Bean's court, and he told them all that they could make up their own minds about what they wanted to do, stay or go back to Mexico.

He was surprised by the response.

"So we what?" Autry asked. "Ride out to meet them?"

"That's right."

"Outside of town?" Piper said.

"Yes," Clint said, "and outside the county."

"When?" Harker asked.

"Now," Clint said, "or they'll come back."

"But . . . we had them fooled with all the guns, right?" Piper asked.

"We did," Bean said, "but that Montoya, he was losing his temper. I think he'd come back in shooting."

"We can't let that happen," Clint said.

"Then," Harker said, finishing his beer, "we better get mounted."

Clint turned to Judge Roy Bean and extended his hand.

"Thanks for the help," he said.

"Well," Bean said, "I tried to help."

"I know," Clint said. "But this is for the best."

"If you live through this," Bean said, "come back and let me know, will you?"

"Sure."

"We'll have that steak," Bean reminded him.

Clint smiled, and followed the others out of the saloon.

After Clint, Piper, Autry, and Harker had ridden out of Langtry, Leroy came into the saloon. Judge Bean was still standing at the bar, holding a beer.

"Leroy."

"Judge."

"What's on your mind?"

"Well . . . I rode out like you told me, Judge, watched the Mexicans ride out," Leroy said. "I thought you'd like to know what happened."

"I would," Judge Bean said, "very much. Come have a beer and tell me about it."

FORTY-FOUR

Clint and the mercenaries rode out of Langtry, reined in soon after.

"How far out will they be waiting, do you think?" Harker asked him.

"The county border," Clint said. "Judge Bean told him how far it was."

"And you're gonna tell us?" Piper asked.

"I am," Clint said, "but I don't think we should ride up on them together."

"Split up?" Autry asked.

"Four ways?" Harker said.

"Yes," Clint said. "I'll just keep going, but you three can circle around."

"Okay," Piper said, "now how about you just tell us where we're circling around to?"

"You can't blame them," Francisco said.

"I can," Inocencio Montoya said, "and I do. They are family, and they are supposed to stand with family."

"They're cousins," Francisco said, "second and third cousins at that."

"Still . . ."

"We have enough now," Francisco said, "to do the job."

"Yes," Montoya said, "we do . . . or we should."

"He's coming, *señor*," Del Plata said.

"What?"

"Clint Adams," Del Plata said. "He's coming . . . alone."

Montoya looked, and saw.

When the group of Mexicans came into view, Clint was surprised. Their numbers had dwindled considerably.

He counted as he approached.

Montoya, his son, Francisco, his two sons, Del Plata, and his five men. Eleven. Quite a difference from the twenty-five they had come with. Clint doubted that Montoya had sent the family home. It was more likely they all decided to go back to Mexico. That probably made him a very disappointed man.

However, with eleven against five, the odds were still in the favor of the Mexicans.

Clint looked around, saw the other men, his mercenaries, approaching from the other three directions. But the attention of the eleven Mexicans was solely on him.

Which was good . . .

"Spread out," Del Plata instructed.

His men obeyed, but the Montoya family stood together, clustered around their patriarch, Don Inocencio.

Bad move.

Or good?

Clint rode up to them, stopped about twenty feet away.

"Surprised to see me?" he asked.

"Surprised to see you alone, Señor Adams."

"Well," Clint said, "it looks like you lost a few people, too. Family decide to go home?"

"They did," Montoya said, "and I will take care of

them when I return. But I have enough men here to do the job."

"So do I."

Montoya frowned, but when Clint gestured, Montoya looked around, as did Del Plata.

"*Conyo!*" he heard Del Plata mutter.

"Señor Montoya," Clint said, "you and your brother still have time to make sure your sons do not die."

"If they die, they die for the family," Montoya said.

"No," Clint said, "they die because your son, Juanito, was stupid. Pablo?"

Pablo Montoya's head jerked as Clint said his name. His eyes went wide.

"Do you want to die because your brother was a fool?"

Pablo swallowed.

"And you, Señor Montoya," Clint said to Francisco. "Do you want to lose your sons because his son was a fool?"

Francisco looked at his two sons, who were looking very frightened at that moment.

"Inocencio—" Francisco started to speak.

"*Basta!*" Montoya snapped. "Do not listen to him."

"Papa—"

Montoya turned his head and glared at Pablo.

From the corner of his eye, Clint saw Roberto Del Plata draw his gun, and then his men followed.

"Okay," he said, and drew his own weapon.

Piper, Harker, and Autry were in place, also twenty feet from the group. All they had to do was make sure they didn't catch any cross fire from each other.

But they were pros.

They wouldn't miss like that.

Clint's first bullet took the top of Roberto Del Plata's head off. The other fighting men were hurriedly drawing their

weapons, but in close fighting like this, they were no match
for the American mercenaries. They were used to fighting
at a distance, or from ambush. Inocencio Montoya had hired
the wrong men.

The Montoya family froze. Francisco spread his arms about
to keep his sons from drawing their weapons.

Inocencio Montoya drew his weapon, his face contorted
by hatred. Clint had no choice. The last shot he fired killed
the patriarch of the Montoya family, and christened a new one.

It grew quiet.

"Drop your guns," Clint said.

"Please, *señor*," Francisco said, "do not fire."

"You're the new head of your family, *señor*," Clint said.
"Tell your sons and your nephew to drop their guns."

"*Baja tus armas*," Francisco said, waving his arms.

The three young men dropped their guns to the ground,
as did Francisco. Clint noticed that Pablo was bleeding from
an arm wound. He didn't seem to notice, though. He bent
over his father's body.

"Papa," he said.

"I'm sorry," Clint said.

Nobody acknowledged his apology.

Piper, Autry, and Harker moved among the bodies, and
then came over to Clint.

"They're all dead," Harker said.

"So is Montoya," Clint said.

"Is it over?" Piper asked.

Clint looked at Francisco.

"Is it over, *señor*?"

"It is over," Francisco assured him.

"Then take your family home."

Francisco nodded. He and the boys lifted the body of
Inocencio Montoya onto his horse, and then they headed for
Mexico.

"What about these boys?" Autry asked.

"We'll bury them," Clint said.

"They deserve it," Harker said. "They were fighting men."

"When we're done, we'll go back to Langtry and spend the night," Clint said.

"That Judge Roy Bean," Harker said, "he's kind of crazy, you know?"

"Oh yeah," Clint said, "I know."

"They got a bank in that town?" Piper asked. "That Langtry?"

"I don't know," Clint said, "but if they don't, or if I can't get the money there, we'll go to Fort Stockton. Don't worry, boys. You'll get paid."

"We ain't worried," Piper said.

Harker looked at Autry, who nodded and then said, "Naw, we ain't worried at all."

Watch for

A DIFFERENT TRADE

396th novel in the exciting GUNSMITH series
from Jove

Coming in December!